"I WANT YOU TO STAY."

He pressed his body into hers, covering her shock-parted lips. Her quickened breath, the feel of her ribs expanding in the circle of his arms, her heart hammering in time to his excited him—so did the fact that she stayed.

He didn't want to stop. It was late, the house was quiet. A moan deep in a woman's throat, a series of ragged breaths wouldn't be overheard. They had time. Privacy.

She caught her breath. He stole it again. "I've wanted this from the day I saw you." He skittered his lips across hers, then opened her with his tongue.

"We shouldn't," she whispered.

"We shall."

WHAT ARE *LOVESWEPT* ROMANCES?

They are stories of true romance and touching emotion. We believe those two very important ingredients are constants in our highly sensual and very believable stories in the LOVE-SWEPT line. Our goal is to give you, the reader, stories of consistently high quality that may sometimes make you laugh, sometimes make you cry, but are always fresh and creative and contain many delightful surprises within their pages.

Most romance fans read an enormous number of books. Those they truly love, they keep. Others may be traded with friends and soon forgotten. We hope that each LOVESWEPT romance will be a treasure—a "keeper." We will always try to publish

LOVE STORIES YOU'LL NEVER FORGET
BY AUTHORS YOU'LL ALWAYS REMEMBER

The Editors

Loveswept® 718

A MAN'S MAN

TERRY LAWRENCE

BANTAM BOOKS
NEW YORK · TORONTO · LONDON · SYDNEY · AUCKLAND

A MAN'S MAN
A Bantam Book / December 1994

If you would be interested in receiving protective vinyl covers for your
Loveswept books, please write to this address for information:

Loveswept
Bantam Books
P.O. Box 985
Hicksville, NY 11802

ISBN 0-553-44461-1

Published simultaneously in the United States and Canada

Bantam Books are published by Bantam Books, a division of Bantam Dou-
bleday Dell Publishing Group, Inc. Its trademark, consisting of the words
"Bantam Books" and the portrayal of a rooster, is Registered in U.S.
Patent and Trademark Office and in other countries. Marca Registrada.
Bantam Books, 1540 Broadway, New York, New York 10036.

PRINTED IN THE UNITED STATES OF AMERICA

OPM   0 9 8 7 6 5 4 3 2 1

ONE

"Balloons!" Five-year-old Aurora shouted in amazement.

Melissa Drummond stood beside her in the doorway, gripping her tiny hand. Together they gaped at the aqua and silver balloons filling the hotel suite. Some butted against the gilded plaster on the rococo ceiling. Some rolled tiredly along the Persian carpet. Others, tied to pots of flowers, bobbed at eye level.

"We'd need a machete to cut through these," Melissa said. "Or a pin," she muttered under her breath.

Aurora raced to the center of the room, kicking up a storm of aqua clouds. No matter how she fought it, a corner of Melissa's heart instantly warmed to the man who'd gone out of his way to put a smile on the face of a little girl he'd never met.

Unless, of course, the thoughtful act was intended to impress the child's mother.

As if in response to an imaginary flourish of trumpets, Helene entered. One arm stretched gracefully from beneath her fur-lined cape, Aurora's mother stood framed in the doorway of the suite. "My goodness, my dear, have you ever *seen* such madness!"

Melissa bit back a smile. The Countess Helene St. Eugenie von Schloss Thuringen, former wife of Prince Albrecht, more recent former wife of Alain Trenchement, the French oil-tanker magnate, certainly knew how to make an entrance. Not to mention a headline. News of Helene's recent pursuit of a new husband had actually bumped the British royal family from the tabloids. Aristocrats from all over Europe vied for the hand of the multimillionairess and socialite.

Some more imaginatively than others, Melissa thought, eyeing the extravagant display. Spotting a note dangling from a balloon, she untied it and handed it to the countess.

"Why, it's Reggie," Helene exclaimed.

Reginald Hempton-Smythe, Melissa silently filled in. Title: Lord Darby. Nationality: English. Estates: extensive. He'd recently become one of the pack of suitors hot on Helene's trail. Helene was equally hot on his, judging from how strenuously she'd ignored him at the Paris Opera the previous week. By the end of the performance he'd practically nipped at her heels.

"That explains the aqua and silver," Melissa replied, nodding toward balloons that bobbed and nodded back. "Those are the colors of his racing silks."

Helene tapped the note to her powdered chin. "He's one of the finest horse breeders in England. Or so I've been told."

Told by Lord Darby himself, Melissa concluded. From what she'd seen of him, the perfectly earnest, perfectly dull landowner seemed bent on merging his bloodlines with Helene's as soon as possible.

In a flash, Helene made up her mind. "We shall go."

"To?"

"To Bedford House. He's invited us for a week's stay. Be a dear and pack, will you?"

Melissa caught the invitation Helene tossed to her as the countess sailed toward the bedroom, shutting the door firmly behind her. Balloons caromed off the wall. In another corner of the room, a little dancing tornado giggled her way through a floating playland.

Melissa felt a twinge for the child's unfailing optimism and innocence. Moving around Europe for the last three years hadn't been easy on the girl. Melissa had been the only steady element in Aurora's life. As part of her duties, she'd tutored her charge in all the basics. But the five-year-old would have to be enrolled in a regular school soon, and that meant her mother had to settle down. Somewhere.

Running her fingertips over the engraved invitation, Melissa found herself wondering if Reginald Hempton-Smythe might be the answer. If the balloons were any indication, at least the man had a sense of humor. And he seemed truly smitten by Helene. Was it too much to ask that he like her little girl too?

She closed her eyes, recalling all the men who'd so carelessly ignored Aurora. Bright and eager, she'd raise up on tiptoe as they approached, anticipating some form of attention at last—only to have it effortlessly stolen by Helene merely stepping into the room. Melissa knew from her own childhood how those slights stung. The day she'd taken the job she'd vowed Aurora would never feel neglected or ignored no matter how much attention men lavished on her mother.

"It's all right," Aurora had explained once in her unnervingly mature way. "Mummy needs a husband. When she has one, *then* I'll have a new daddy. I just need to be patient."

What did a five-year-old know of patience? A child needed someone to make her feel special, unique, loved. But Melissa's instructions were clear; she had packing to do and reservations to make. Before beginning any of it, she called the little girl's name.

Aurora ran to her, her arms filled with balloons. "Yes, miss?"

"We're going to see Lord Darby, the balloon man. Would you like that?"

Instantly cautious, Aurora thought before answering. "I will, if he likes me."

Melissa went down on one knee and hugged her hard. "He will, puppet. I know he will. If he doesn't, he's full of hot air!" Giving Aurora a conspiratorial wink, she yanked a balloon down from the ceiling and poked it with the invitation's folded edge. It popped with a bang.

Aurora squealed. In seconds, the room sounded like the inside of a popcorn machine as balloons burst left and right.

Melissa gaily popped another one. Let that be the fate of anyone who'd toy with the affections of a little girl to gain the hand of her wealthy mother!

She swept the shriveled remnants of a dozen balloons from the desk and dialed the concierge. According to the invitation, they need only appear at England's Heathrow Airport on Thursday morning. Lord Darby's man, Reilly, would have everything else in hand.

❖━━━━━━❖

By the time they reached Heathrow, Melissa's skeptical mood had drowned in a sea of details. Breathless and harried, she secured their baggage. Scanning the precise instructions Reilly had faxed to Paris, she directed their luggage to Pad One, whatever that was. Crossing off the last item on her list, she trod to the farthest gate at Heathrow. There she found Helene and Aurora staring serenely out a plate-glass window.

Coming up behind them, Melissa caught sight of her disheveled reflection and stopped in her tracks. Her shoulder bag had tugged her ruffled blouse over to one shoulder. She'd covered it with a bright red deep-V pullover that draped to her thighs. That was askew too. The off-white stirrup pants were wrinkle-proof, ideal for comfort and ease of movement.

She didn't look at ease. She looked exhausted. Her freckled cheeks were flushed. Curly tendrils of red hair splayed across her forehead like the limp tails of a dozen leaky balloons. Her mother would have had a fit. "You'll never catch a man's eye looking like that."

Probably not, Melissa thought. But after Sally's five marriages, Melissa was determined to have other goals in life. So what if she was exactly what she appeared to be— a nanny, a secretary, and a traveling companion? She busily saw to all the details that made Helene's life blissful and carefree.

Nevertheless, comparisons struck her every time she glanced at her elegant employer's perfectly applied makeup and designer clothes. Helene's ebony hair swept to her shoulders in one long wave, unlike Melissa's, which coiled and twisted like untended vines.

Sighing, Melissa despaired of ever acquiring such effortless poise. "If wishes were horses, we'd all be Lord Darby, breeding them by the dozens."

Helene turned without looking directly at her secretary. "What was that?"

"I've followed Lord Darby's instructions, ma'am. We should be met momentarily."

"Good." Helene nodded at the landing pad, a red-and-white target painted on the ground. "Did you realize we were taking one of those?"

Melissa searched for the limousine and driver.

Aurora tugged her hand. "We're taking a whirlybird."

"A helicopter," Helene corrected, tilting her head as she weighed the word. "Do you think he leases it?"

Melissa gulped. Squat and dark green, the helicopter sat on the landing area like a frog on a lily pad. Inside its wide-open doors, the leather seats were a familiar shade of aqua. "There's a family crest painted on the tail," she said in a shaky voice.

"So there is." Helene's opinion of Reginald Hempton-Smythe rose dramatically.

Melissa's stomach plummeted. She hated flying. In the three years she'd handled their travel arrangements, they never flew in anything less than a massive international carrier. This *thing* had all the birdlike grace of a garden slug wearing a beanie propeller.

She caught sight of a man circling it, headphones slung around his neck, pea-green jumpsuit zipped shut. The pilot. She fought a desperate urge to tap on the glass and ask if he might drive them instead. His intense concentration told her he wouldn't be easily deterred from taking off as planned.

She was about to take off, straight down the concourse. Her heart stuttered like a faltering airplane engine. Her lungs struggled with stuffy recycled air. Her hands grew damp at the very idea of high altitudes. No two ways about it, the family-crested eggbeater was a nightmare come true. So was Helene's enthralled expression. Melissa would never get the socialite on a train now.

Very well, her conscience commanded, she could handle it. She got to airports with time to spare for exactly this reason. It gave her a chance to check out the pilots, white-haired gentlemen oozing authority in gold-buttoned uniforms.

The man in the zippered jumpsuit was age thirty-five at best. His hair: sandy brown, short and neat. His skin: weathered and creased—by a deep-seated sense of responsibility, she hoped. Add to that his broad and reliable shoulders and a back unbowed by any signs of fatigue, and Melissa felt a trifle more composed.

Until he turned and caught her staring. In a face that revealed little emotion, his golden-brown eyes were the gentlest she'd ever seen.

Melissa held her breath as he walked toward them. His precise stride would have seemed stiff and formal on anyone else. On him, it seemed natural and relaxed, like a man who always knew where he was going, who never faltered or hesitated. A man to rely on.

He opened the door and curtly bowed his head. "The stairs are in place. You may board."

"Thank you," Helene replied, sailing regally past him.

"You, too, lass. All aboard."

Aurora raced after her mother, her teddy bear clutched under her arm.

Melissa remained rooted to the spot.

"Not afraid of flying, are you, miss?"

Afraid? Only of letting it show. All her life she'd earned her keep by being as little trouble as possible.

Gait stiff, head level enough to balance books on, she strode onto the tarmac. The whine of jets, the bustle of mechanics, and the acrid smell of petrol greeted her. Ten steps ahead, Helene climbed the portable stairs and took her seat in the helicopter's belly. Aurora scampered up behind her, bounding next to a window.

Melissa hesitated. She swallowed. Her shoes stuck to the tarmac. The pilot resumed his preflight inspection, making check marks on his clipboard. She used his presence as an excuse to remain outside, studying him as acutely as he studied his machine.

He walked around the helicopter's nose, absentmindedly splaying his hand on the machine's metal skin, petting it the way a groom steadied a skittish horse. Melissa imagined that touch, she clung to the warmth and comfort it conveyed. She pictured it against her skin, calming her, steadying her.

Their eyes met. She straightened, afraid he'd misinterpret her look. He neither presumed nor accused, but calmly accepted her scrutiny. For a fleeting moment the glimmer in his eye said he even welcomed it.

A rivulet of heat trickled beneath her skin. She shuddered and crossed her arms over her breasts, blaming their tight buds on the damp English day. She felt flushed and chilled at the same time, dizzy, queasy. Alarm bells went off all over her body. It felt a lot like being aroused. Or airsick.

She nearly laughed out loud. The sound died in her throat as the pilot closed the distance between them. His clipboard tapped lightly against his thigh. He let her look her fill.

She plucked at the ruffles of her collar. "This English weather!"

"Too cold or too hot?"

"A little of both really." She rubbed clammy palms the length of her sweater. Slapping them together, she took a deep cleansing breath.

He said nothing. His eyes said it all. He'd wait all day if necessary.

Absurdly grateful for his patience, she gave him her most apologetic smile. It felt cockeyed. *She* felt cockeyed. She was back to being seventeen again, all elbows and knees and gangly limbs. "Crazy, isn't it? People fly every day."

He shook his head slowly. "Some people never leave the ground."

Melissa knew exactly what he meant. Some people never took a risk, never left their comfortable worlds no matter what their mode of travel. The understanding formed a bond between them. It was also an unspoken challenge. Amiably but unmistakably, he was daring her to take a chance.

On the helicopter or him? she wondered.

She averted her gaze, nodding at his clipboard. "Are you sure there's fuel in the tank?"

He tapped his pen against the paper, making a note in the margin. "Glad you mentioned that."

She furrowed her brow, the better to glare at him. "I sincerely hope you're joking."

He squinted, scanning the helicopter from the ground up. "Air in the tires, check. Windows washed, check." His gaze lingered on the very top. "Yep, the wings are on."

A shocked laugh broke free. Melissa surrendered. "I'm sorry to be such a worrywart. I'm sure you know what you're doing."

"I do." He said it softly, with all the steely conviction she'd already glimpsed. "I never make a move without knowing exactly what to do and how to do it."

"Does that apply to women too?" Her cheeks flamed the minute the words left her mouth. She couldn't believe she'd said that.

Apparently he could. He looked a little deeper.

For a stunning second all the hubbub ceased. The whine of jets faded to a distant buzz like riled bees trapped in giant tin cans. A humming sensation whispered beneath Melissa's skin. She felt suspended in air thick as honey, captured in his amber gaze. All her life she'd wanted someone to look at her that way, as if he really saw her, as if how she felt mattered.

She shook the moment off, giving him another crooked grin. Flirty games were fine for people who played them. Helene would have known just what to do.

"Forget I ever said that. Nerves, I guess." Compared with making a fool of herself in front of a total stranger, the helicopter looked more inviting by the second. She gestured woodenly at the stairs. "Time to go, Mister . . . ?"

"Reilly. At your service. And miss?"

"Yes?"

"I like your nerve."

She laughed, a halfhearted puff of air. Breathless, almost buoyant, she climbed the steps, Reilly following close behind. A frisson of sparks raced up her arm when he touched her elbow.

"It's perfectly safe, miss. I'd never take a child on board if it weren't."

Aurora. Melissa latched onto the child like a lifeline. Not for the world would she convey her misgivings to the little girl. Crouching beneath the low ceiling, she sidled over to her. Maybe, if she asked very nicely, Aurora would share her teddy bear during takeoff.

Reilly's low voice stopped her in her tracks. "Sorry, miss. You'll need to sit up front with me. To balance out the load."

She veered toward the copilot's seat, sinking into the stiff leather. Reilly took his place beside her. Plugging in his headphones, flipping switch after switch, he spoke quietly and efficiently to the person on the other end.

The regular clicking sound revealed how often he'd done the same routine things. His methodical thoroughness told her he took none of it for granted. The engine droned as the droopy propeller rotated, picking up speed.

Melissa dragged her gaze from the safe solid earth. "I hope you don't mind if I stare."

Reilly's mouth quirked in a purely male grin. He knew full well she'd been doing it all along. However, his manners remained above reproach. "Whatever makes you feel at ease, miss."

Getting hormonal notions out of her head would be a good start. The man was competent, clearly experienced, and so totally self-assured, he teased her about her fears. "The wings are on, my foot," she muttered to herself.

She was the one fantasizing about competent hands

caressing flesh, about an experienced, methodical man making love to a woman. She was the one daydreaming about someone so completely self-assured, he'd tease a woman right out of any self-consciousness she might have in bed. *Whatever makes you feel at ease. Miss.*

She felt like a total ninny. She never indulged in romantic fantasies. She'd seen her mother chase after too many of them, trading in husband after husband at the first sign of waning passion. Which is what passion inevitably did, Melissa thought coolly as the helicopter shuddered and lifted off the ground.

"You really know how to sweep a woman off her feet," Melissa thought of saying. The joke lodged in her throat, directly beneath a thick knot of pure terror.

TWO

Bracing herself, Melissa gave Reilly a fierce stare. His alert eyes scanned the tarmac. She followed them, spotting fuel trucks and taxiing airplanes, jet commuters and SSTs. They were in the middle of a giant three-dimensional chess game, and only Reilly knew exactly where all the pieces were.

When her jaw unclenched, she shouted over the roaring engine. "How far to Bedford House?"

He nodded to a set of headphones mounted on the copilot's side. While she put them on he reached forward, twisting a knob on the control panel. His gaze traversed her face, resting on her eyes before falling slowly to her lips. "Can you hear me?"

Her heart thudded. His disembodied voice sounded intimately close, murmuring directly in her ear. Barely a foot away, she watched his lips move as he turned up the volume and asked again. "Can you hear me?"

She flicked her tongue across dry lips and nodded.

"Speak into the microphone if you need me."

What she needed was a good stiff drink. She fiddled

with her microphone, hoping he couldn't hear her shallow breathing. Blades whirled violently outside her window, spinning themselves into a smudged gray blur. She focused on the one stable, physically solid element in the vicinity.

He had narrow lips, Mr. Reilly did. He pursed them when he concentrated, drawing them into a fine line when he surveyed the area. She wondered how they'd taste. Not that she'd ever find out. He was intriguing, so relaxed and severe at the same time, soothing and distant at once.

She wondered about his background. Military probably, judging from the crisp way he handled his duties. That would explain where he learned to fly a helicopter. And where he'd gotten the scar. The jagged mark started at his hairline then wound its way along his right temple, disappearing beneath the headphones.

He twisted around, pulling the microphone down from his mouth to speak to Aurora. "Ready to see London from the air, lass?"

"I've seen it," the child replied quite honestly.

"In a jet," Melissa explained. "She's a seasoned traveler."

"What about Sherwood Forest, then?"

Aurora's mouth dropped open. "Where Robin Hood lives?"

"Aye and all his Merry Men."

"I'd love to!"

"We pass over Nottingham on the way to Bedford House. I'll show you all their hideouts."

Aurora immediately pressed her nose to the glass.

Reilly settled back with a grin. Melissa caught his eye. "Thank you," she said softly. "For everything."

He drew a pair of dark sunglasses from his pocket, grinning devilishly. "Thank me when we land."

Relaxed at last, she laughed at his gallows humor. But frivolity switched to terror when air currents jostled them. The helicopter bobbed like a giant balloon, hovering one hundred feet off the ground.

Helene yawned, flipping the pages of a fashion magazine. Aurora clapped her hands. Melissa covered her mouth.

She sent a longing glance Reilly's way as they headed due north. She needed to see the teasing glint in his eye, the steady surety of purpose that told her everything would be all right. But nothing reflected in his dark glasses except a wide-eyed redhead gone extremely pale.

"Everything all right, miss?"

"Fine." Except that she missed him all of a sudden, and she didn't know how or why. As he scanned the skies and chatted with the tower, she felt unaccountably left out. It was an old feeling, being the outsider, a pain as familiar as a toothache. She refused to nurse it. She was there to keep an eye on Aurora not pine after pilots. She twisted around in her seat.

A strong male hand closed on her arm. "Okay?"

"Just checking."

He checked on the little girl himself then glanced at Melissa as if reminding her of what he'd said. *I'd never take a child on board if it weren't safe.*

Maybe there were men in the world who cared about a little girl's feelings, she thought. And maybe little girls weren't the only ones who needed them.

Nonsense. Reilly would soon be gone. He'd set them down at an airport somewhere and be on his way, flying off like a helium-filled balloon. Or like love itself whenever a woman was foolish enough to believe in it.

A nervous one, Reilly thought to himself, glancing at Melissa an hour and a half later as they zeroed in on Bedford House. The sooner they landed, the sooner she'd relax. Maybe he'd get a flash of the smile she'd tried so hard to give him on the tarmac at Heathrow. It surprised him how much he looked forward to it.

Truth to tell, she'd hardly taken her eyes off him the whole trip. He could flatter himself by thinking it was his looks, but lying to himself was something Reilly never did. He was simply a man doing his job. If he did it well, she'd thank him profusely once they touched down, and they'd both be about their business.

It was a routine he knew well. The restless sense of wanting more bothered him. A faint trace of perfume teased his senses. He knew it was probably the countess's scent. All the same, he enjoyed imagining it emanating from this woman's skin, a soft fragrance that hovered around her like the delicate hairs on a woman's belly, that glow of gold his hands might skim.

His hand tightened on the throttle. She tensed. She was as aware of him as he of her, but for different reasons.

He nodded toward the square of bright green meadow cut into the forest three hundred yards from Bedford House. "We'll land there."

"Great," she replied. She stared straight ahead, eyes fixed, lips pressed tight.

He laughed to himself. He liked her. She hadn't let the fear win. While he'd spun stories about Sherwood

Forest for the little girl, the attractive nanny had joined in, laughing, questioning, debating his wilder inventions. All the while she'd gripped the armrests until the leather dented beneath her short fingernails. She wouldn't show the little girl a lick of fear, but she couldn't hide it from him.

The curse of being a trained observer, he thought. He was also a man; the image of those nails digging into his shoulder blades made him press his back against the seat.

Hyperaware of everything around her, the nanny imitated his motion, as if some tremendous G-force was about to push them backward. No need to worry. He'd set them down as easy as one would a baby in a bassinet —or a woman on a bed.

In the meantime, Melissa shifted her lean legs, crossing one tightly over the other. Her face was pale and oval-shaped, her eyes an anxious blue. Her constant gaze betrayed an unearned trust in his abilities, a readiness to believe in him.

He, on the other hand, placed his trust in things he could feel, taste, touch. Not for him, unearned faith in others. He'd tried it before with disastrous results.

He purposely slackened a bitter frown. *Just do your job.* He had a reputation for keeping his cool. There'd been a time when he'd been called downright cold. Heartless.

He pointed out the meadow below. Inside the green square grew a massive oak. Beneath it spread a tiny white square. "This is it, miss."

"That isn't what we're landing on!" she declared.

"No, ma'am. It's what we're eating on."

"A picnic!" Aurora shouted.

"A picnic?" the countess asked, leaning across her daughter for a better view. Astounded and amused, she chuckled to herself. "Reggie is *so* inventive."

"Aye," Reilly muttered to himself. "He has a romantic streak as big as all outdoors."

Melissa caught his remark on the microphone and looked sharply across the cockpit.

Reilly kept his face impassive. Treetops fluttered directly to his left. Melissa's hand clenched the armrest to his right. Without asking himself why, he reached over and unwound her fingers, wrapping them with his around the throttle.

"What are you doing?" she demanded.

"Bringing her in." He scanned the field from side to side.

"Melissa's landing the plane," Aurora exclaimed.

"Oh no, she isn't!" Melissa shouted directly into the mike.

Reilly winced inside his headphones. "I wanted you to have a sense of control, miss. It makes it easier if you're involved." That applied to a lot of things men and women did together.

Keenly aware that the little girl watched their silent tug-of-war, Melissa whispered fiercely into her microphone. "I can't do this."

"Sure you can. Easy as shifting a car."

"I drive automatics."

He grinned, his grip unrelenting. There was no danger; she couldn't move the throttle if she tried. Nevertheless, rumbling vibrations coursed through their linked hands. Her trembling and the machine's mixed. His heart beat steady as a clock. "Ready?" he asked.

She stared wide-eyed as he pressed his fingers between each of hers. The scent of perfume grew, heightened by her heated skin. His skin heated in response. Her breathing grew sharper, shorter; her breasts rose and fell inside the baggy sweater. He imagined them palm-sized and pink, unsupported by any bra, molded by a man's hand. It was all tactile now.

His eyes focused elsewhere while hers remained fixed on him. She'd look at him that way in bed, as keyed in on his reactions as he'd be on hers. They'd climb the way this machine had, a breathtaking stomach-dropping lift or a slow-rising glide until—

A thudding sensation shuddered through his body. He gave a final glance at the controls, the fantasy doomed to remain unfinished. "We're here."

She yanked back her hand the moment he released his grip, darting a panicky look at the deserted controls. She gaped at the grass outside the window. "We've landed!"

He pulled off his headphones, raking his fingers through his hair. "That's what I said, miss."

"But all I felt was a little thump! I thought it was—"

He looked up when she stopped short. "And what kind of thump would that be?"

Melissa sat back smartly. Never you mind, she thought. Her careening emotions were her business. Why they'd chosen to ricochet from bad memories to fruitless fantasies was something she'd consider later in the privacy of her own room. By then their pilot would be long gone.

If only the quivering remnants of her fantasy would fade that fast. She'd pictured their bodies entwined, his hands firm and knowing, his body thrumming like the helicopter, encasing her, swooping down on her, his shaft as hard and slick as that throttle. Her hand would close around it as his had closed on hers, showing her exactly what he liked, what he needed.

She needed fresh air.

She unbuckled her seat belt, wheeling in her seat. She focused on the real reason she was there. "Wasn't that wonderful, Aurora?"

The little girl chattered a mile a minute while the rotor's motion died down. Melissa scooted back to pick up her stuffed toys and unread storybooks. "We'll read *Robin Hood* tonight."

"I saw his house!" Aurora exclaimed. "We flew right over it!"

"I know we did." Melissa knew full well those could have been any woods. Still, she was grateful to Reilly for playing travel guide. He'd pointed out Robin Hood's exact address, telling tall tales in such a matter-of-fact way he'd had the little girl mesmerized the entire trip.

Her nanny had been mesmerized too. But for entirely different reasons.

Reilly opened the doors and set out the staircase. She couldn't wait to put her feet firmly on the ground.

Helene descended first. "Where is Lord Darby?"

"He'll be arriving shortly, ma'am."

She extended her hand to Aurora. "We're going on a picnic, darling."

"Yes, Mummy."

"I assume you'll be expected to participate. You must be on your best behavior."

"Yes, Mummy."

"When the main course is done, Melissa will get you your dessert."

"Yes, Mummy."

Melissa understood the unspoken command. The countess wanted a little private time with Lord Darby toward the end of the meal.

Without another word or backward glance, Helene proceeded across the field to the picnic area. Aurora hung back.

Melissa knelt swiftly, searching through her shoulder bag for a comb. She drew it through Aurora's honey-blond hair, stifling a moan as flyaway strands insisted on living up to their name. "It'll be fine, princess."

Her little chin sank to her chest.

Melissa lifted it with the flat of the comb, looking her straight in the eye. "Lord Darby is a man of taste and discernment." *I hope.* "If he has any sense at all, he'll think you're the best little girl he ever laid eyes on."

Aurora cast a dispirited look after her mother. Her chic pencil-thin skirt barely hampered her stride as she crossed the park. She tossed her glimmering ebony hair in the afternoon sun. Aurora sighed. "He won't even see me."

Probably not, Melissa thought. When Reggie caught sight of Helene, the little girl wouldn't stand a chance. "He might be preoccupied today. After all, he hasn't seen your mother since—since Sunday. But I promise, before the week is out, he'll look at you and think to himself, 'Where has this pretty little girl been all my life?' "

"Honest?"

Melissa hated making promises she couldn't keep, but what else could she say?

To her immense relief, Reilly came to her aid. "Aye, lass. Any man with eyes to see would think himself blessed to have a daughter like thee."

Aurora brightened, hanging on Reilly's every word. After all, this was the man who knew where Robin Hood lived.

He bowed from the waist. "If there's anything else you need during your stay, just ask for me."

As if asking would get Aurora a father, Melissa thought.

But Reilly had a magical way of reassuring people. Aurora drew on his quiet confidence. Giving him a solemn nod, she squared her small shoulders and marched after her mother.

Melissa watched her go, silly tears stinging her eyes. At times like this she knew she'd invested too much of herself in a child who wasn't her own. But for all her genuinely good qualities, Helene was simply too involved in her topsy-turvy love life to pay Aurora the kind of attention she needed. Maybe when things settled down, when Helene found a husband who truly loved her, and children too . . .

"If wishes were horses . . ." Melissa sighed.

"Pardon me, miss?"

"Nothing." She sagged against the helicopter, watching Aurora take a tentative seat on the far edge of the picnic blanket approximately sixty feet away.

Melissa knew all too well what it felt like to be a third wheel. Dragged from one of her mother's romances to another, her childhood had been spent not messing things up for Mama. On her best behavior at all times, she'd impressed Sally's latest flames with her manners, her good grades, and her art projects. But the talent that came in most handy seemed to be her ability to disappear when the adults didn't want her around.

Aware of Reilly busying himself inside the helicopter,

Melissa contemplated how kind he'd been to Aurora. For that she owed him her thanks. It would be unspeakably rude to give him the cold shoulder simply because she found him incredibly sexy. He was an enigma, rough-edged yet cool as polished stone.

An enigma with warm, faintly callused hands, she thought, rubbing hers briskly together. She turned when he rejoined her. "Mr. Reilly—" She gasped.

He'd peeled off the flight suit. Beneath it he wore a butler's white shirt with a gray-striped vest and black floppy tie. She gaped as he shrugged into a black coat, the tails flapping.

"Are you the butler too?"

"I manage the estate, miss."

"But you fly."

"And oversee the groundskeepers and the security mechanisms. We have staff, of course, but times being what they are, manpower is stretched a bit thin."

Melissa knew from paying Helene's bills how tight the times were. With her extravagant lifestyle, the multimillionairess wouldn't be multi for long. However, if one of Helene's criteria for marriage was financial security, she'd be very interested in hearing about Reggie's servant situation.

"Do you think a lack of staff might harm Lord Darby's suit?" Reilly asked cautiously. "Might it hamper the courtship?"

He'd read her thoughts. Before she could compose a suitably benign response, he'd pulled a picnic basket from behind a seat. What seemed like dignity and poise on the helicopter now struck her as chilly aloofness. Did he imagine Helene as some gold digger out to land a sugar daddy? Was he silently judging them?

A sense of protectiveness surged through her. He had no idea what Helene had been through in her marriages. "According to certain perfectly awful tabloids," Melissa declared hotly, "it might appear that Helene is only after money. I'm sure she cares very much for Reg —I mean, Lord Darby—or else we wouldn't be here."

"For my part, miss, I believe he cares for her," he answered mildly.

"Does he?"

"Naturally, he doesn't confide all his feelings to me."

Embarrassed at her ardent defense, Melissa slanted her back against the helicopter. The metal skin was cool. Hers remained flushed, her breasts tender and heavy, the nipples scraping against her blouse. She tried not to think about it. "Naturally, the countess hasn't confided all her feelings to me either. However, one might safely assume that she hopes to find what any reasonable woman wants in a marriage."

"Which is?"

"Love. Mutual respect. Commonality."

"Commonality, miss?"

"Having things in common."

"Ah. Like estates? Property? Resources?"

She had the irritating sensation he was baiting her. "If you insist, yes."

His eyes met hers for a long moment. "I never insist."

Her retort caught in her throat. She had the strange sensation they weren't talking about Helene anymore, or marriage. Without either of them mentioning it, by the subtlest of means, he let her know exactly what he meant. It was as if he could read every tingling nerve zinging beneath her skin, as if he'd placed his fingers on her racing pulse.

She searched for hints of teasing in his eyes, but he'd turned back to his work, calmly unwrapping a wedge of cheese. He'd said all he needed to say while barely saying a word.

Irked, off balance, and not at all sure why, Melissa surveyed the inside of the picnic basket. It didn't look like the kind of meal with which one would impress Helene. However, to say so would make her sound like a snob and only reinforce Reilly's apparently low opinion of them.

Trying to pick up the conversation where it had fallen apart, Melissa felt compelled to remark that financial security was an understandable concern wherever great fortunes were involved. It sounded perfectly reasonable in her head. Coming out of her mouth, it sounded unutterably pompous. "There's Aurora's future to consider too. A good mother always thinks of her children's well-being."

"I'm sure she does. She hired you."

Melissa blinked at the unexpected compliment.

"It's my understanding the child's father was a prince," Reilly said.

"By birth and title but that's about it." The subject of Aurora's no-account fathers always got her hackles up. Despite their genealogies and impressive bank accounts, neither man had had any sense where children were concerned.

"I was hired after Helene's marriage to the prince collapsed," Melissa said, deciding Reilly could learn the same information from any supermarket tabloid. "The divorce settlement took years to work out. By then

Prince Albrecht had had a son by his *next* marriage. He pensioned Aurora off with a trust fund. He shows no interest in her beyond that. As for her stepfather, Helene's second husband, Monsieur Trenchement, he had no use for children whatsoever."

"You and the child must have spent a lot of time together."

"We do."

"Are you afraid that will change if her mother remarries?"

His insight impressed her. She repaid it with honesty. "I'm afraid she'll get her hopes up and her feelings hurt."

"You care about her very much."

She folded her arms protectively. She'd never spoken to anyone about her job. No one had ever asked. Reilly's patient stillness seemed to invite intimacy. Caring, whether genuine or not, could be dangerously seductive. "I've been running on, haven't I?"

"Nothing untoward, miss. The excitement of the day."

He didn't seem excited. His bland expression was completely unreadable. Did anything ever shake Reilly?

She appraised him with a glance as he worked. He wasn't much taller than she was. She was five foot eight and thin as a rail, a lanky Yankee if ever there was one. He was no more than five ten, a sturdy broad-faced Yorkshireman judging from the clipped accent that occasionally slipped into his speech. He flew helicopters and spread pâté with the same methodical attention to detail. She studied the scar again. Unhidden by headphones, its ugly progress trailed from hairline to temple. Intriguing didn't begin to describe the man who wore it.

"Have you worked for Lord Darby long?"

He glanced up, peering over her head at a path in the woods. The purr of an automobile engine detached itself from the twittering birds and sighing breeze. "That will be His Lordship now."

A black Rolls-Royce emerged from the forest, gliding into the clearing like a yacht sailing into port.

"Helene's not the only one who knows how to make an entrance," Melissa muttered.

"Thank you, miss."

"Pardon me?"

Reilly bit his tongue. It wasn't his place to reveal he'd thought up all these circus tricks. Balloons, picnics, helicopter rides. What did he know about wooing women? But Reggie had practically begged him to come up with something to impress the countess.

No one had warned him about Melissa. The smitten Reggie had mentioned a little girl and a nanny. Reilly assumed she'd be a sturdy, middle-aged, no-nonsense woman carrying a tightly rolled umbrella and wearing comfortable shoes.

Never assume, his army training scolded him. So did that other immortal bit of common sense, *Never volunteer*. He'd promised Reg he'd do what he could to impress their guests. Never once had he pictured Melissa among them.

Her smile beamed like the sun breaking through clouds. She had a gangly coltish build and fiery hair. Orange-red curls bounced all around her face, sassy and pert, with a mind all their own. The woman had an equally feisty nature, a store of courage that bent but didn't break, and a heart that bled for neglected little girls. For Aurora, Melissa's arms would always be open.

Not for you, he reminded himself. Observing her reactions to his mildly risqué double entendres, he knew she wasn't the kind to welcome a fast affair. Not that he sought one. If Reggie's courtship didn't work out, Melissa and her mistress would be gone within the week.

And if it did? If he accomplished everything Reggie asked of him, the countess might stay on. The premarital arrangements necessary to merge and protect two family fortunes would take months. There'd be a wedding, a child in the house—and a nanny to look after her.

"You're counting your countesses before they're hatched," he told himself with a grim smile. Lord Darby wasn't exactly the Prince of Wales. A thirty-five-year-old bachelor steeped in horse breeding and country living, he could be dull, stuffy, shy, and retiring. When he was unsure of himself, which was most of the time, he spoke as if his mouth were full of marbles, covering up his nervousness with long-winded speeches. Spontaneity was not his strong suit.

Decency was. Reginald Hempton-Smythe was decent to the core, in Reilly's humble opinion. He was too good a man to be taken for a ride by some high-living socialite. But would the Countess Helene St. Eugénie von Schloss Thuringen wait around long enough to find out how kind he really was? Did she care?

The freshly waxed Rolls glided to a stop beside the picnic blanket. The chauffeur hopped out and opened the rear door. Reilly subtly stood to attention. A woman's body obliterated the view as Helene launched herself into Reggie's arms.

Reilly winced. It was painfully obvious the gentleman was unused to being inundated with feminine affection. He shuffled his feet. He backed up. He didn't know where to put his hands. Reilly had the sinking feeling he would have patted Helene on the head if her arms hadn't wrapped around his neck like a noose.

Reggie patted her back instead. There, there.

Reilly pursed his lips and looked to the sky, muttering dire imprecations. *Good Lord, man, kiss her.*

The countess received a peck on the cheek. Reilly suppressed a groan.

Suddenly a tiny movement caught the corner of his eye. Melissa wrung her hands, her eyes fixed on Aurora. As the child hung back, waiting to be noticed, Melissa's head bobbed, sending signals of silent encouragement. "Go on," Melissa whispered. "Say hello."

To his consternation, Reilly found himself muttering the same instructions to his employer. "Go on, man. Walk up to the child. Smile a bit. Take her hand."

After an uncomfortable pause, Reggie noticed Aurora. He stepped forward stiffly. He stuck out his hand and gave her a firm pat on the head. Aurora whipped out the bear she'd been hiding behind her back. Stumped momentarily, he patted that too. Aurora seemed satisfied. Reggie smiled.

Melissa and Reilly sighed in unison.

THREE

Melissa blushed. They sounded like two cooing doves!

Reilly coughed into his fist. The countess took a seat, leaning languidly against the tree trunk. Reggie took up a rapt position beside her. Aurora played with her bear on the blanket's corner. The chauffeur, Miller, performed exactly as planned. Setting a wine bucket on the grass, he opened a box lined with crystal goblets and set it down. Then he humbly retreated to the Rolls and backed it down the path until it disappeared into the trees.

Opening salvo fired and target objective reached, Reilly thought.

"Would it be out of line to ask how Lord Darby feels about children?"

Melissa's question stopped him cold. He got the sense she'd ask anything on behalf of the little girl. He wondered if she asked anything for herself?

"Children," he repeated, stalling for time. He rocked slightly on his feet, clasping his hands behind his back as he studied the ground. "Lord Darby is a bachelor, miss."

"Mm-hm."

"He doesn't number many children among his acquaintance."

"Mm?"

Before he could think of a better way to put it, a movement on the picnic blanket seized his attention. Reggie had inserted the corkscrew in the wine bottle. Wrestling manfully with the magnum, he managed to get it in a headlock between his elbow and his side.

Melissa folded her arms and cocked a brow, observing the scene with a wry smile. The man was no Alain Trenchement, that was for sure. To give him his due, he probably had efficient and able servants to perform such tasks. People like Reilly.

The butler and sometime pilot had gone quiet beside her. Watching him out of the corner of her eye, she glimpsed his left hand clenching and unclenching as he silently directed his master in how to uncork a bottle of wine.

The thump of a cork sounded across the clearing. Helene's gay laugh trilled on the same air. Reilly's hand relaxed. Melissa timed her sigh to match his. Startled, he shot her a look before turning firmly back to his work.

She chuckled as the Rolls magically glided back into view. A cadre of servants stepped out one after another, like circus clowns. Aurora looked completely enchanted. Helene looked suitably impressed. Melissa looked at Reilly.

He scanned the staff from a distance, noting how they comported themselves. Each carried a silver tray or a small picnic basket. They took turns serving various courses before obediently withdrawing.

Like a field general pleased with the progress of a battle he'd orchestrated, Reilly nodded to himself.

A sudden realization struck Melissa with all the oomph of a popping cork. "You arranged all this!"

His face became completely impassive. "It's my job to see that things run smoothly, miss."

A nonanswer if she ever heard one. From what she'd seen of Lord Darby in Paris, he was entirely too dull to woo a woman in such a way. Reilly, on the other hand, was the soul of organization and imagination—not to mention discretion.

"I mean all of this," Melissa insisted. "Flying us in, landing in a field, having a picnic."

"Is something not to your satisfaction, miss?"

As a matter of fact, there was. Her eyes narrowed. "You never did say whether Lord Darby likes children."

"Didn't I, miss?"

She huffed. Getting information out of him was like wringing gourmet mustard from a stone. She crossed her arms, tapping her fingers against her biceps. Although the English couldn't abide nosiness, she had Aurora's interests to look out for. "Does he? Like children, I mean."

Reilly handed her a plate.

She munched a watercress sandwich, pinning him with an unwavering glare. "Well?"

"Lord Darby appreciates his horses, his gardens, and Bedford House."

"In that order?"

He ignored her flippant tone. "He may not be particularly warm or given to outward signs of affection, but he's not a cruel man. He's—careful."

"Meaning what exactly?"

"He takes care of what's his."

Melissa pictured a massive country house filled with perfectly preserved museum rooms, the kind little girls couldn't raise their voices in. "Perfect gardens? Perfect breeds of horses? Perfect everything?"

Reilly gave her a steady look. "He's a good man."

For some crazy reason, she believed him. That didn't mean she couldn't make judgments of her own. She observed the threesome at their picnic until the dishes were cleared away. That done, Lord Darby rose and escorted Helene toward the forest's edge. As they strolled into the deepening shade Helene curled her arm through Reggie's arm. He gave her hand a pat.

Reilly groaned low in his throat.

Melissa glanced over. "Where are they going?"

"Over the hill is a small pond stocked with goldfish. After they see that, he'll show them a stand of oaks planted in King James's time."

"Aha!" Melissa pointed an accusing finger at Reilly's chest. "So you *do* have this all planned!"

Butter knife swiping a piece of bread, he stopped in midmotion. "It's good to be prepared, miss."

"Scripted is more like it."

"Are you always this suspicious?"

"Only where love, or men, or both are concerned."

"Don't you want everything to go smoothly for your mistress?"

"Adults can take care of themselves. Aurora's happiness is what matters to me."

"And your own?"

The question stopped her cold. Why should he care? And why did she secretly long for that kind of caring?

He studied her, his gaze coolly dropping from her

face to her breasts to her waist, the long span of her legs. She was frozen in place, aware of her breasts pushed up by her tightly crossed arms, her stomach tensely pulled in, her knees knocking. She pressed them together, abashed to see him smile faintly. He shook his head as if to say, "What a waste."

Indignant, Melissa flushed and stared brazenly back. Let him survey her like a stretch of runway. The longer he looked, the more opportunity she had to examine him —that square stubborn jaw, the rare strands of white gold in his sandy hair, the shocking gentleness of his eyes when they again rested on hers.

Once more he let her look, not shy, not bold. He was there if she needed him. But she didn't want to think about that, about needs opening inside her, a long-standing loneliness she was usually too busy to think about. She scanned the field for Aurora.

The little girl had veered away from her mother and her beau. She ran pell-mell toward the helicopter. Melissa instantly held out her arms. "Are you okay, puppet?"

Seeing Reilly, Aurora abruptly slowed to a walk. Shrugging, she stared at the grass, dangling her teddy bear by one arm. "They were talking boring talk."

"Ah."

She accepted Melissa's kiss then wandered over to see what was on their plates. Without thinking, she reached up and took Reilly's hand.

"Did you thank Lord Darby for the luncheon?" Melissa asked, a twinkle in her eye.

"Yes."

"I think you should thank Reilly too. He arranged it."

"Did you arrange the balloons also?" Aurora asked.

Melissa laughed, astounded at the child's insight. "You did, didn't you!"

Reilly confessed—somewhat. "I hope they weren't overdone, miss."

"They were marvelous." Melissa grinned. "Helene liked them and Aurora adored them."

"Did *you* like them?"

She blinked. Just when she thought they'd be comfortable acquaintances, he treated her as if her opinions mattered. As if she mattered.

"They were simply lovely," Aurora stated, unconsciously mimicking her mother's Continental drawl.

Melissa chuckled and the tension vanished. She *liked* Reilly, there was no getting around it. If they were going to be working in close proximity for a week, it'd be easier to face that fact head-on.

While Aurora gripped his other hand, Melissa brazenly wound her arm through his. "The balloons were just right," she declared. "I expect everything you do is just right."

"I try, miss."

"Now show us this pond of goldfish."

He bowed and led the way. Strolling through the trees, he related the story of Bedford House. At one point he covered Melissa's hand with his. Part of her wondered how she'd become so accustomed to its warmth in such a short time. Another part warned her not to get too attached. This was Helene's love affair, after all.

Reilly's subtle distance sent an unmistakable signal. He wasn't the least bit interested in her. For that, she was sincerely grateful. It said she could relax with him.

To borrow a British expression, the man was safe as houses.

Of course, some houses were safer than others, Melissa thought later that evening as they dined with Lord Darby. Although dying of boredom might not be most people's idea of a life-threatening condition, she was deeply worried about succumbing to utter tedium. Lord Darby had taken full advantage of Helene's adoring looks to launch into yet another detailed explanation of the European Economic Community's grain negotiations. It seemed he was on a committee. . . .

Raising her eyelids before they fell permanently shut, Melissa contemplated the ceiling towering over the dining hall. Plaster moldings framed an unused chandelier. The walls were a rich dark red on which lacquered oil paintings covered every inch of available space. Marble busts of noted ancestors stood guard in recessed corners. Melissa felt sorry for them; they *had* to keep their eyes open.

Helene laughed gaily. Melissa's head snapped up. She focused on the flickering candlelight, the soft golden glow surrounding the wall sconces. It was all terribly romantic. Probably all Reilly's doing. She just couldn't stay awake.

Somewhere in the massive hallway a clock chimed eleven. She stifled a yawn, peeking at Aurora. The child's chin had sunk to her chest. Melissa expected a soft snore at any minute.

Then she caught sight of Reilly, standing in the shadows by the wall. Her heart gave a thump. Her temperature rose as the level in her wineglass sank. Why?

she wondered. He'd stood there all evening, the soul of propriety. He directed the staff, stepping forward whenever Lord Darby signaled for more wine, perhaps a bowl of sherbet for the little girl. He was totally attuned to everything that went on, the unacknowledged master of all he surveyed.

Would he be masterful in bed? Melissa thought, the wine heating her from the inside. Would he be controlling? Directing? Or would he serve, attuned to a woman's every need?

She gulped the wine, aware she'd been rolling the hot liquid on her tongue. Chasing such nonsense from her mind, she kept her wishes simple. She would love to talk to him some more, trading good-natured gossip, talking shop, relating to him on a professional level, stopping this man–woman stuff before it went any further.

Lord Darby's story stumbled to a stop. He signaled Reilly.

"It'll be seen to at once," Reilly replied.

After Reggie's drone, the sound of his voice disturbed her. Some part of her had been hearing it all evening, the faint Yorkshire accent, the way he called her Miss. "I took the liberty of putting flowers in the countess's rooms," he'd said this afternoon. "Is she allergic to any?" The man thought of everything.

So why couldn't she stop thinking of him? He hovered on the edge of her awareness the way he waited on them, discreet, aloof, always there.

He stepped beside her, a bottle of sherry in his hand. "Would you care for any, miss?"

"No." She jumped to her feet. Everyone turned. "Excuse me. I think it's time I put Aurora to bed."

Aroused by the sound of her name, Aurora gave a sleepy-eyed nod.

Reilly pulled Melissa's chair out. She stepped away from the table, her legs shaking. Before he guessed at her own baffling reactions, she had to get out of there. She nodded to Helene. "Good night, ma'am. Good night, Lord Darby."

"Oh, but wait," Reggie announced, dismayed to see his audience evaporating. "I wanted to tell you all one more story."

Aurora rubbed her eyes, mumbling. "Is it about Robin Hood?"

"It's about Reilly."

Melissa instantly came awake. She sensed the butler behind her become subtly tense.

"Is that entirely necessary, sir?"

"Nonsense, old man. They'll love it."

Helene leaned forward. Her silver lamé evening gown draped elegantly from the spaghetti straps crossed over the golden expanse of her tanned shoulders. "But Reg, darling, I thought you were going to tell us a little of your family's fascinating history."

Reg looked disappointed. His suggestion hadn't exactly been joyously received. "But it's a good story."

Reilly addressed the countess. "Actually, ma'am, I believe this story *is* family history."

Melissa pondered the long-suffering tone Reilly tried so hard to disguise. Beneath his impassive demeanor he seemed downright ill at ease. He hadn't arranged this part. "A story about Reilly," she murmured, grandly taking her seat. "I can't wait to hear it."

Aurora plopped back into her chair.

Resigned, Reilly marched to his place along the wall and stood with his hands clasped behind his back.

"Well then!" Reggie rubbed his hands together. "I was attending to some business of Her Majesty's government in Northern Ireland. Nothing of major importance, mind you, but part of my duties for a subcommittee in the House of Lords—"

Reilly discreetly coughed into his fist.

Reggie blinked. "Ah. Anyway. One morning, as I got into my automobile—I didn't have a driver at the time, or rather, the one I had remained here at the estate—"

Reilly raised himself on his toes, bouncing lightly.

Reggie got to the point. "I opened the car door, slid into the driver's seat, put my key in the ignition, and there, on the wheel, was a note. 'Warning,' it read, 'if you start this automobile, it will explode.'"

"No," Helene exclaimed.

"Yes." He scanned the faces around the table. "I was further instructed to use my car phone to telephone my London bank and transfer one million pounds to a specified account. If I didn't follow these instructions, my Jaguar and I would cease to exist in precisely thirty minutes—or whenever I opened the door."

Helene gasped. "How perfectly dreadful. What on earth did you do?"

"I called Reilly. Or rather, a branch of Special Services. The Bomb Disposal Unit."

It was Melissa's turn to gasp. "You were in bomb disposal?"

Reilly's eyes caught hers briefly before veering back to the middle distance. "Previous career, miss. Didn't last long."

"Long enough for me," Reggie quipped.

"Indeed," Helene purred. "Please, do go on."

He colored from his collar to his ears as her fingers insinuated themselves between his. "Twenty army men and three armored vehicles arrived. While they examined every inch of the Jaguar Reilly stepped up to the window, tapped on it with his knuckle, and said, 'Excuse me, sir, could you spare a moment?' "

Everyone grinned. Melissa took advantage of the moment to study Reilly.

"Not sure whether I should lower my window or not, I asked him if it was safe? And do you know what he said?"

"What?" Helene, Melissa, and Aurora asked at once.

" 'We'll soon find out, sir.' "

They burst out laughing. Even Reilly smiled briefly.

"What did you do?" Helene asked.

"What could I do?" Reggie answered. "Since the man himself seemed willing to stand there while I tried it, I gave it a go. I turned the handle—" He indulged a dramatic pause.

Aurora's eyes grew wide as tea saucers. "And?"

"And?" Melissa asked, blood rushing in her ears.

"Nothing. Absolutely nothing. Reilly handed me a handkerchief to wipe my forehead then announced they'd located the bomb beneath the bonnet. The car's hood," he amended for his American guest's benefit. "While everyone took up positions behind their vehicles Reilly opened his tool kit, set out a selection of wire cutters, and got to work. He could have been a mechanic fixing my carburetor, for all the fear he displayed. He talked during the entire episode, telling jokes, commenting on the weather. Heavens, I can't remember half of what he said now."

Reilly responded to his cue. "Just making conversation, sir."

Reggie harrumphed. "After twenty-eight minutes, mind you, twenty-eight of the thirty promised in the note, Reilly stood up, slapped the dirt off his hands, and opened my car door as if he were a seasoned chauffeur. I tumbled out like a limp rag, I can tell you."

"You did all right, sir," Reilly filled in. "Tough job, relying on others."

"But I had you to rely on, Reilly, that's the point." He turned to his breathless audience. "There and then I offered him a position for life. Seeing as he'd just saved mine, it seemed only fair."

"And he accepted on the spot," Aurora declared.

"Oh no." Reggie frowned. "That's the funny part. He declined. One year later to the day he shows up on my doorstep. 'I'd like to join your service,' he said. Isn't that right, Reilly?"

"Or words to that effect, sir. You remember it better than I do."

Melissa doubted that very much. There didn't seem to be anything Reilly forgot or overlooked. Curiously, the fact that he'd once led a very dangerous life didn't surprise her. That he'd replaced it with such a bucolic one fascinated her immensely. Why would such a man go into household service? The story raised more questions than it answered.

But none of them would be answered tonight. As Helene cooed over Reggie's narrow escape and Aurora yawned, Melissa pulled back her chair. "Time for bed, puppet."

"But I want to hear another story."

"Some other time. Now kiss your mother good night."

Aurora did as she was told, suffering through another pat on the head from Reggie. Reilly opened the door to the hallway. The little girl hesitated on the threshold.

"What's wrong?" Melissa asked.

"Are there bombs upstairs too?"

Reggie bolted upright in his chair. "Good Lord. Have I frightened the child? I never meant—"

"It's fine," Melissa assured him. "She's in a strange house, and it's well past her bedtime."

Reilly took charge of the small crisis. "I'll see her to her room, if you don't mind, sir. The staff will clear away later."

"Indeed. Good man. You do that. I'll handle everything on this front." He nodded somewhat stiffly in Helene's direction.

"There's a fire in the library and some brandy set out if you and the countess would care to retire there."

"Splendid," Reggie exclaimed, immensely relieved. "You really do think of everything."

"Just doing my job, sir."

Reggie offered the countess his arm, and they strolled down the hall toward the library.

When they were gone, Melissa mused out loud. "Why do I get the idea you'd say you were 'just doing your job' even if it involved saving the Queen of England from a herd of rampaging buffalo?"

Avoiding her teasing grin, Reilly hefted Aurora's sagging little body into his arms and carried her up the staircase. "You could be right, miss."

Melissa glowered at his back. After one day's acquaintance, he remained a complete enigma. " 'You could be right,'" she muttered. "And if pigs had wings, they could fly."

"I wouldn't know about that, miss." He paused at the door to Aurora's room.

"You don't miss a thing, do you?"

"I try not to."

"Is that the bomb-squad training?"

He carried Aurora to the bed, tenderly setting her down. "Will you be sleeping in here, miss?"

She knew darn well he hadn't answered her question. There was no use his playing the butler with her. She'd seen the man beneath the disguise, the humor, the insight, the intriguingly rough edges of someone who wasn't to the manor born. Someone like herself.

"I'm in the adjoining room," she said.

"Ah." He stepped back as Melissa unbuckled Aurora's shoes. "Won't the child be afraid if she wakes in a strange house alone?"

"Not a chance. When this one's out she's out for the duration."

"Very good, miss."

"Thank you for asking, though. You're very sensitive, you know that?"

"I've been called worse."

"By whom?" She caught a flash of something long hidden in his eyes.

"I'll be going, then."

"Reilly?"

"Yes, miss?" He stopped halfway to the door.

She knew he'd evaded all of her questions so far. She knew she had no right asking them. And yet, there were so many things she wanted to say. She crossed the room to him, stopping inches away. There were depths to him she hadn't begun to figure out, secrets that compelled her. "That was quite a story."

"He enjoys telling it."

"And you enjoy seeing him happy."

He shuffled his feet. "If you don't mind my saying so—"

"Yes?" She stepped closer.

"They might make a good couple."

"They?" She didn't mean it flirtatiously. She was enthralled, that's all, bewitched by the glow of the bedside lamp transforming itself into distant fires in his golden-brown eyes. She couldn't fathom what he'd been through, or what had brought him there. Why did he flirt in the helicopter and keep his distance in the house? And why, without her knowledge, did her hand reach out to bridge the distance between them?

Because it was the only way to reach him. Words hadn't worked, and he was a man who needed touching.

Her fingertips skimmed the side of his face, tracing the raised outline of a scar. Sympathy flooded through her. He would have gotten it there, in Northern Ireland, a bomb—

He gripped her wrist.

She gasped softly.

"I'm sorry, miss. I don't get involved with the guests."

"Involved? I—"

"I don't get involved where I don't belong. If you don't mind my saying so."

She didn't know what to say. Heat rushed to her cheeks. "I didn't mean—"

"I'm sure you didn't, miss. We'll leave it at that, then."

"I'm sorry." Her exclamation caught him in the doorway.

"No need to apologize, miss. I suspect it's high time we were both in bed. I mean— Well, good evening." He closed the door behind him.

It should have been funny, the way he caught himself on his own double entendre, flustered instead of flirting. It would have been funny if she hadn't felt like the world's biggest fool.

FOUR

Whatever possessed her to touch the man? Days later Melissa blushed to think about it. She hadn't meant it as a romantic overture. She'd just meant—

She sighed. She wasn't sure what she'd meant, except that behind that distant facade seemed to lurk a man with more facets than he cared to show. A lonely man.

And an attractive one.

But that wasn't any of her business. She had Aurora to see to. The child had an entire house to explore. Apparently she intended to see it all in one day. "Honestly, Aurora. You act as if this is a giant dollhouse."

"It's fun."

It was also a wonderful way to avoid any more embarrassing encounters with Reilly. Melissa set to it. All day Friday and Saturday she and Aurora crept through countless attics, brushing away cobwebs, discovering antique prams and high-button shoes. They were wonderfully lost when Aurora tugged a bellpull in a deserted bedroom on the third floor and Reilly magically appeared. The child imperiously demanded he unlock a mysterious door. Melissa demanded her heart stop beating like a wound-up clock.

He looked marvelous, his ruddy cheeks freshly shaved, his hair glinting in the mote-filled sunlight, his shoulders broad in his black tailcoat. The muscles of his abdomen were flat and firm inside his striped vest, Melissa noticed as he smoothly produced a skeleton key from his waistcoat pocket.

He opened the oddly shaped triangular door beneath the sloping roof. "Watch your step, lass."

Melissa's eyes darted to his, but he seemed to have meant the words solely for the little girl. Aurora entered the attic as if it were a magic cave.

Unfortunately, tricky steps were the least of Melissa's worries. She hung back while Aurora poked around inside. She knew she should seize the opportunity to offer an apology for the previous night's impulsive touch. It amazed her how many ways she'd rehearsed the words. Suddenly none of them fit. Her mouth tasted of hundred-year-old dust.

"Did you need me for anything else?" he asked, filling the strained silence.

Was it her overworked imagination putting a suggestive twist to his every word? Or her underused heart? Yes, she needed him for something else, for friendship, someone to talk to. The words created a sudden ache in her throat. She found the courage to say them. "I thought we could be friends."

He concealed his mild surprise. He hadn't expected her request.

Served him right, she thought. She never knew what to expect. One moment he was a pilot, the next a butler, a bomb disposer, and always a sexy mysterious man.

"We'll be working together for a week. Living in the same house—"

"You're a guest, miss."

"It's not as if a gaping social chasm divides us. I'm a fellow employee. We can relate on a professional level at least."

"At least," he murmured, a trace of disapproval in his dry tone.

"Honestly, you've been treating me like fine china. Some table that needs polishing."

"Have I, now? It was my understanding I'd barely touched thee." He remedied that, his fingers gliding from her shoulder to her elbow, pressing the fine knit of her sweater.

It was as if the heat of his fingertips communicated directly to her skin. She shivered everywhere.

The touch had the same effect on his voice. It grew raspy, his accent thick. "You're a woman who could use touching."

She'd once thought the same of him.

"Your skin would glow. The way it is now." He lifted his hand from her shoulder to her cheek, brushing back a tangled strand, caressing her with the barest tips of his fingers. It was enough. He found her ear, dropping to the sensitive skin beneath it.

Too much. She shuddered and stepped back. She'd been playing with fire, unlocking doors to places she didn't understand. Her whole muddied purpose had been to make a friend, not invite intimacy. "I'm sorry if you misunderstood."

"I'd be surprised if I had." His eyes brooked no argument. He'd known what she meant that night, and why she stayed now. He knew why her feet remained planted as he skittered his fingers the length of her neck.

Her body swayed. She felt light-headed, breathless, betrayed by the longing hidden in that simple contact. "Friends," she whispered. She wouldn't ask for anything more. She didn't believe in anything more.

His hands dropped obediently to his sides. He bowed. "If you need me for anything else."

"I won't."

He handed her the key, placing the warm metal against her palm. "This opens many doors. Feel free to use it for as long as your stay." His gaze held hers.

Like a tart sip of lemonade, the teasing glint in his eyes brought her back to reality. She gripped the key until the teeth bit her palm. "Can it lock doors too?"

"If you wish."

He wasn't letting her back out so easily. She should have known. Reilly was a man with a passion for details. He'd see to her every need—if she let him.

A childish exclamation drew her attention. She breathed a sigh of relief. "Aurora."

His stare didn't waver. "She's safe in there."

But was Melissa safe out here? "I have to find out what she's getting into. They get into everything, you know. Rusty nails, ancient bear traps."

For a moment she wondered if Reilly would accept her lame excuse. He let her pass.

Stooping beneath a rafter, she felt the denim of her jeans pull taut across her behind. Sensations tingled through her like fireflies. She imagined Reilly watching from the doorway with that quiet, soul-scouring thoroughness of his. He saw right through her to needs she'd long denied.

She refused to think about it. She had Aurora to see to. Her willful little charge lurked in there somewhere. She swiped at a cobweb, wishing she could break through the web of mystery surrounding Reilly the same way. Afraid she already had. Where did he come off announcing she needed touching? Or that he was the man to do it?

She'd heard similar proposals in her time, usually from Helene's impatient suitors, wealthy men who arrogantly assumed a nanny was an extra added attraction, or a consolation prize. She wasn't there for a fling. Somewhere along the way, distracted by fear of flying, intrigued by Lord Darby's story, she'd let her curiosity about Reilly convey the wrong impression. Next time, she'd make it perfectly clear.

"Boo!" Aurora leaped out from behind a chimney.

Melissa nearly jumped out of her skin. She grasped a sooty little hand in hers and headed for the door. She'd tell Mr. Never-Bat-an-Eye Reilly exactly how slim their chances for involvement were.

But he was gone.

See? She badgered herself silently. It was all your imagination. It was his job to be polite to her, to be attentive. To come when called. *If she rang the bellpull beside her bed tonight, would he appear there too?*

She huffed and dragged Aurora into the light of day, locking the attic door securely behind them. That was one fantasy she would not entertain.

But he touched you.

Because I touched him, she thought furiously. "We've put that behind us now. We're even."

"But we can go back if we want, can't we?" Aurora's wide blue eyes pleaded with Melissa's stern frown.

Melissa heaved a sigh. "I was thinking out loud again, wasn't I?"

Aurora peeked over her shoulder. "The attic *is* behind us."

"Then let's keep it that way!"

By Saturday afternoon, Melissa had nearly put her disturbing encounter with Reilly out of her mind. Reilly obviously had. Touring the stables with Helene and Lord Darby that morning, Melissa caught sight of him walking from the garage. She smiled politely. He nodded back. His posture was perfect, his expression formal, remote, thoroughly uninterested.

Just the way Melissa wanted it. Like the suits of medieval armor displayed in the west wing, his attitude protected her from any silly fantasies. Although it irked her a bit that he'd decided to ignore what had happened before she'd had a chance to insist he do just that.

By Sunday afternoon, peace and goodwill descended on Bedford House with a vengeance. Aurora and Melissa played in the nursery, attended chapel, ate brunch, then came outside to ramble through the gardens.

While Aurora danced through the herbs and carefully tended paths, Melissa sat on a cement garden bench in the tepid English sunshine. She luxuriated in the feel of sun on her skin, brushing her cheeks with traces of color. Gentle breaths of air whispered through her hair.

It was Reilly's warmth she envisioned, his breath on her cheek, his hands caressing her skin until— Her eyes snapped open. Two baby-blue eyes stared at her.

Aurora pointed. "Let's look in there."

Melissa twisted around to look at a wall of high greenery.

"Come see!" Aurora skipped off and disappeared around the far end of the hedges.

Sighing, Melissa followed. More activity might chase Reilly from her thoughts. She strolled to the hedge's end, expecting another garden on the other side. Instead she entered a long shaded corridor. On its left a solid wall of branches grew. On the right three openings beckoned.

"It's a maze!" She grinned and stepped inside. How appropriate. She'd been going in circles ever since she came to Bedford House. It didn't matter what made Reilly tick. In four more days she, Helene, and Aurora would pack up and find another country house, another lord or magnate or marquis.

White gravel crunched beneath her shoes. She reached a dead end, hedges on three sides. Retracing her steps, she found another opening and picked up her lecture where she'd left it off.

Naturally Reilly appealed to her. They were birds of a feather, living their lives on the edges of other people's lives, efficient, independent, alone. That's why his brazen demonstration of desire unsettled her. She'd thought him safe, reliable, remote. The way everyone else seemed to see him.

Aurora ran by up ahead. Melissa smiled. At least she had the little girl. Aurora would always have someone to love and depend on.

Who cared for Reilly? Melissa wondered. Why should she worry about him? He had this entire house to look after. For a girl who'd been dragged from new home to new home, Melissa envied him that sense of belonging. He'd never been as adrift as she had, as lost—

"Speaking of lost." She turned in a circle. Every path looked the same. She listened for the soft crunch of Aurora's skittering footsteps. "Aurora?"

A giggle floated through the foliage. Melissa turned another corner. She walked faster. Two openings gaped on her left, one lured her farther on the right. She peered around the first and saw a wall of green and a stately marble urn. "Where are you?"

"I'm right here," Aurora answered with impeccable logic.

"If you're there, where the heck am I?"

A giggle and a flurry of stones. Melissa looked both ways then cheated. Parting the branches with her hands, she stuck her face in the opening. No good; the hedges were ancient, thick, and high. Tiny branches clawed at her cheek. She pulled her head out as newly trimmed leaves fluttered to the ground.

She turned east then south then west. Eventually she came to a fountain where an angel quenched the thirst of another with a flagon of burbling water. She'd seen it three times already. "Aurora?"

The giggles grew fainter. Her little angel enjoyed this tremendously. After another ten minutes of fruitless searching, Melissa seriously wondered if she'd get out in time for dinner. The sun slipped behind a wall of clouds, the air turned decidedly chilly. Slanting shadows darkened the maze.

Gravel crunched on the next path over. She ducked beside a green archway as the steps grew closer. Counting to ten, she let out a piercing cackle and leaped. "I'll get you, my pretty, and your little dog *too*!" Arms flailing, she swooped down on her captive five-year-old.

Her head bumped smack into Reilly's abdomen.

He grunted. Regaining his footing, he held her at arm's length—as if she'd butt him again given the chance.

Regaining her composure took a moment longer. She raked a fistful of tangled hair off her forehead. To her chagrin, three stray leaves fluttered to the ground. As if her head sprouted greenery every day, she coolly ignored them. "How did *you* get here?" she asked.

"One of the maids saw you from an upper window. She suggested I lend assistance. Were you looking for the way out?"

She was looking for a hole to crawl into. She was a competent levelheaded woman of twenty-seven. Why was it every time she met Reilly she needed rescuing? "I'm perfectly fine, thank you."

He glanced her up and down, taking his time on the way up. "I agree with you there, miss."

Blood rose in her cheeks. "I was admiring your, uh, shrubbery."

"Is it to your liking?"

"It's very dense."

"Ah." The teasing gleam faded from his eyes like a curtain dropping. He indicated the path. "Would you care to follow me?"

She'd like to give him a swift kick in the pants. He acted as if guests disappearing in the maze were an everyday occurrence. She trailed him down one lane after another. "I could have sworn I tried this path."

"It is puzzling, miss. People often get lost and don't know which way to turn."

"Don't go getting philosophical on me, Reilly."

"I beg your pardon?"

She didn't repeat it. She glimpsed a private smile curving his lips as they rounded a corner. The sight made her heart trip. Her feet followed suit.

"Watch your step, miss."

The maze wasn't half as puzzling as the man before her. A firm male body lived inside those formal clothes; she'd rammed her head into it. About as giving as a brick wall, she thought. She longed to ask what brought a soldier to a life in the country but didn't dare. He'd probably put her off by saying he was just doing his job.

"Have you seen Aurora?" she asked.

"Cook is giving her some soup. She emerged several minutes ago."

"Is that a polite way of saying a child could find her way out of there faster than I could?"

Another grin glimmered beneath the surface, a twinkle of humor in his eye. They emerged at the rear of the house. Bowing, Reilly swept his arm toward it. "Here we are, miss."

Indeed, Melissa thought. Coworkers, colleagues, housemates, couldn't they at least talk to each other? Three days of the week were already used up. Never living anywhere for long, Melissa had learned not to get attached. But she'd never been foolish enough to turn down the opportunity to make a friend. They could have a lot in common, once they got past this uncalled-for awareness.

"Seriously, Reilly, thank you for rescuing me. Again." She gave him a snappy salute and turned on her heel. "Couldn't have done it without you."

"Just doing my job, miss."

Her feet stuck to the ground. Her whole body tensed. Her eyes squinched tight, and her shoulders rose toward her ears.

Instantly he stood beside her. "Is something wrong?"

"If you say you're 'just doing your job' one more time, I think I'll scream." Despite her clenched teeth, she prided herself on how reasonable that sounded.

He looked baffled. "I'm sorry, miss. Just doing my—"

She opened her mouth. His fingers covered it.

His touch froze the breath in her lungs. Whatever she'd meant to say, the words vanished under his fingers' steady pressure. So did the friendly mood she'd tried so hard to create.

He skimmed her lips, pausing to outline the swell of her lower lip, pressing gently, reminding her of what he'd said two days before. She needed touching.

Her body rebelled, so did her heart. He couldn't mean that the way it felt, as if he longed to touch someone, as if he'd yearned for this since the day she arrived. But Reilly didn't yearn for anything. Reilly was completely self-contained, aloof, unfeeling.

His eyes said different. Roving from her startled gaze to her upraised chin, they confirmed everything she feared. He needed her every bit as much as she needed him. When he had her it wouldn't be any sophisticated coupling, one heartbeat removed. With Reilly, lovemaking would be intense, no reaction unexplored, every sensation lingered over, relished.

"We shouldn't be doing this." She gestured awkwardly toward the house looming behind them.

"If you say so, miss." Far from agreeing with her, his

soft burr promised so much more. All she had to do was say the word.

"You said you didn't get involved with the guests."

"You said you weren't a guest."

She drew in a shaky breath, dampening her lips with her tongue tip. His thumb tasted salty. For one shocking moment she considered taking it in her mouth. His eyes darkened in response as if reading her thoughts, or her body.

Unnerved, she pulled her head back. "I don't believe in these kinds of affairs."

"And what kind would that be?"

The kind that made a woman's legs tremble. "I don't believe in love."

He chuckled, seemingly more fascinated with the feel of her skin than with her words. "What does believing have to do with it?" He withdrew his hand.

The tingles remained, radiating from her mouth to her flushed cheeks, racing down her veins. "I don't want this," she insisted even as she longed to lean against his firm body, to be enfolded in his arms. Hold me up, her heart cried out, reach for me, and I won't run away.

He clamped his hands securely behind his back instead. "Excuse me, miss. Old habits die hard."

Like wanting someone? Needing them? Her mind whirled. "What habits are those?"

"Saying I was 'just doing my job.'"

"Oh." Her body trembled like a reed on a riverbank, currents eddying around her, liquid heat flowing through her.

"I won't say it again if it bothers you." He promised it so softly, so genuinely.

"Why should you care what bothers me?"

Because he did. She saw it in his eyes.

This wouldn't do. Lust might be buffeting her body, but love— She recovered her senses long enough to give a breathless laugh. "If Helene and Lord Darby don't hit it off, I'll be gone."

"Quite right. Then it's for the best. I wouldn't want anything troubling you during your stay."

"Including wanting you?" She shouldn't have said it. For the life of her, she couldn't regret it.

The facade cracked. All his attempts at indifference failed. With one step, his body brushed up against hers. One hand cupped her waist, the other the back of her neck. He kissed her without preamble, frankly, hungrily. This was no tentative kiss. It was a man claiming his right to be a man. Politeness, protocol, deference ended where that kiss began.

Suddenly it was over. The stirrings of a breeze that could have been his breath whispered over her parted lips. She opened her eyes.

Just as the withdrawal of his fingertips on her lips had shown her how physically real they'd been, so his absence proved how moving his kiss had been. Her reaction kicked in a second late, her heart thrummed, the breath in her lungs was stringy and thin.

He said nothing. Glancing over her head, he surveyed each window on this side of the house, satisfied they hadn't been seen. With a curt nod he indicated the kitchen door. "After you, miss."

After subjecting her to a blatant, bruising, brazen kiss, he expected her to smoothly resume their just-friends charade? Not in a million years. Which was about how long it would take her to forget the taste of him.

Uneven gravel shifted beneath her feet as she lurched toward the back door. She paused in the old stone archway, leaning against the cold jagged stone. "You know we need to talk about this."

"If you care to, miss."

Her eyes flashed at his detached tone. "Of course I care." That didn't come out right. "What I mean is, I wouldn't be saying we had to talk unless we had to. There are certain things we need to face."

"As I said, miss. If you care, we'll talk." He left her standing alone on the flagstones.

Stumped, furious, supremely agitated, Melissa paced around her room. She had to talk to him, and he'd made that impossible. According to his cryptic statement, speaking would be tantamount to declaring she cared for him. What was she supposed to do, spend the next four days using hand signals?

When the tall case clock downstairs chimed eleven, she glanced in on the sleeping Aurora. Another of Reggie's endless dinner stories had knocked the little girl out for the night.

Melissa thought of the bullying dragon in Aurora's favorite bedtime tale. Like the dragon, her desires would dry up and blow away the moment she stood up to them. She and Reilly would talk. They'd dismiss this silly attraction for what it was, infatuation, lust. Love didn't even enter into it.

Striding toward the narrow servants' staircase at the

end of the hall, she smiled grimly and headed down to the dragon's lair.

Moisture rose from the water-filled sink, steaming the lower half of the window. Soapsuds crackled, blending with the crowd noise of a football match ending on the radio. Leeds up two goals on Manchester United. "And the crowd are going wild."

Reilly smiled to himself and set another plate on the drying rack. Although Lord Darby had purchased a dishwasher at Cook's request years ago, there were evenings Reilly needed simple tasks. He'd been over the estate from top to bottom these last few days, seeing to it everything was in place in case Reggie wanted to take the countess on a tour or another clandestine, carefully catered picnic.

He chuckled to himself. Hard to believe he'd been assigned a role in creating this romance. What did he know about women? The words Clare had shouted at him that day in County Armagh summed up his affect on women. "You don't belong here! What did you ever know about it, you heartless bastard? Get out!"

Maybe she'd been talking politics, the intractable problems of Northern Ireland. Maybe she'd been talking about men versus women. It seemed there were some things no amount of love could make right.

He rinsed a gold-rimmed plate and set it beside its mate. As he eased his hands into the soapy liquid, his fingers squeaked over the pale surface of a piece of china. A picture of Melissa came to mind.

He picked up a scrub brush, attacking a dried crust of mustard on a plate. His hand froze. The hair on his neck prickled. In the clear black panes above the blurred window, he caught her reflection. She stood in the doorway, half in, half out, as if she tasted danger too. He concentrated on his breathing, giving himself a split second to think. "Evening, miss."

She pulled back her shoulders and strode inside, a bluff if he'd ever seen one, but a brave one. "I didn't know you saw me."

He set the brush down, drying his hands on a dish towel. "Were you looking for Cook, miss? A snack perhaps?"

"After the feast we had tonight?"

"Cook's very proud of her rack of lamb."

Melissa laughed. He liked her laugh. It reminded him of open air, the private picnic they'd shared beside the helicopter as Reggie wooed Helene and Melissa kept her eyes on the child. Now it seemed like a lifetime ago, before she'd learned to be wary around him, leery of the emotions they pretended weren't there.

The kitchen was a long low-ceilinged room, its plaster darkened by heavy oak beams. She took her time crossing it, dawdling the length of the servants' dining table, her fingers trailing its marred pine. Reilly was damned if he could figure out how a womanly alluring movement like stroking a table could seem so vulnerable and hesitant. And why that vulnerability, that womanly doubt, attracted him even more.

He watched as her eyes darted from the cupboards to the stove, taking in everything except his cautious stance. She nodded to the sink. "I thought that would be someone else's job in a house this size."

He released the towel twisted around his fist. "I like

doing it myself. My mother taught me. She was a council nurse."

Melissa glanced up, openly curious, willing to listen as long as he wasn't talking about them.

He held that look, aware he'd given her very little of himself so far. To do so would mean crossing a line he'd drawn the day he'd come to this house. She was a guest. He had no business with her. He crossed the line without looking back. "A council nurse handles neighborhood cases, people who've come home from hospital but still need care. Whenever she worked late my father cooked and I cleaned up."

"Looks as though you enjoy it."

"It's fine after a long day. A good way to lay your thoughts to rest." He could think of a better way. Having a woman to come home to, someone to love. "Are you sure there isn't anything I can do for you? A cup of tea?" The water would have to boil, the tea brew. She'd have to stay.

She smiled her no-thanks and perched her denim-clad behind on the edge of the table. In a simple silk blouse cut in a V and blue jeans, she looked classy and curiously young. She'd gathered her hair low on the nape of her neck with a droopy ribbon. Tendrils escaped around her long oval face, uncontained, impish.

Her wide grin blinded him to all her other contradictions. She held the table's edge with both hands and leaned forward conspiratorially. "Do you know what I'd really like?"

"What, miss?"

"To know more about you."

"I'm afraid that would be rather boring."

She clamped her hands between her knees. "No, it

wouldn't. You're incredible. A bomb-disposal expert, a helicopter pilot, a butler. A dishwasher."

He snorted. "Some require more skill than others."

They chuckled together. Her hair in this light matched the orange-red glow of Cook's copper-bottomed pots. Her curls danced, even when she grew breath-catching still, her eyes soft and steady on his. "Can't we be friends?"

He'd never be able to stop at that, not once he'd started. He'd told her that. A kiss such as the one they'd shared should have said it all. Apparently she didn't want to hear it.

The woman needed loving, devotion, passion. She wanted "friendship."

He hid a sneer. Turning back to the sink, he plunged his hands up to his wrists in hot water. Patting beneath the suds for something to wash, he gripped a fistful of knives.

"You're good with children," she observed.

The unexpected compliment pleased him. Children were important to her. "Do you fancy them, miss?"

"You mean children of my own?" She shrugged. "I'd have to get married first."

"You don't fancy that?"

"I don't believe in it."

He studied her. She spread her hands in a miniature shrug.

"What about your mistress, then? She's rather intent on marrying."

"My mistress?" Melissa grinned and corrected him. "In America she'd be my employer. Mistresses are something else."

"A man's lover."

"A married man's lover," she said quickly, lest he get ideas.

He had them already. They nagged him like unfinished chores, demanding he set them in order. Sweetheart. Lover. Wife. Which would she be? Or would he think of her years from now as the one who got away? Her life was tied up with whatever the countess did. His anchored here. He'd best keep his mind on his work.

Silence settled over them. Suds burst like radio static. She crossed her ankles, twining one foot behind the other. He kept his eyes on the water, sensing her every move. Like defusing a bomb, he considered the safest action, afraid the least mistake would set her off and she'd be gone.

They were a man and a woman, alone in a kitchen at night, not exactly a life-or-death situation. "This is nice." She nodded at the kitchen. She was determined they could be friends.

"You've never been here before."

"Not in the kitchen."

Yes, she had. He'd imagined her sitting across the table from him, sipping tea as the house settled down around them for the night, becoming part of his life, necessary, real.

He tried to imagine her gone, the room haunted by her memory. The way Clare's taunts haunted him still. *You don't belong here!*

He belonged at Bedford House. He'd worked for it. He didn't want to lose it by doing something stupid.

"Why the frown?"

He glanced up from his chores. "Nothing, miss."

She seemed content to watch as he worked. He wished to hell she'd go away. If she didn't, he might start believing what his instincts shouted. She belonged there. She belonged with him.

She tilted her head. He noted the tightness in his chest when she smiled at him in the window's reflection. She was a beautiful woman. When she was with the child, her loving nature beamed like sunshine. Around others she hung back, self-effacing, competent, seeing to everyone else's happiness. Who saw to hers?

He did. He would.

Deep down, his intensity amused him. He was leaping with no idea where he'd land. No matter. Loving a woman was like defusing a bomb. One made up one's mind and acted. He'd often bet his life on the snip of a wire. He followed his instincts when they fairly shouted in his ear; he'd regret it the rest of his life if he let her go. But how to hold on to her?

An obvious image came to mind. He'd grip her body close to his, kissing her, taking it farther, deeper this time. If he'd read her correctly, he could predict how she'd react. And how she'd run afterward.

There seemed to be only two ways to make her stay. Either he kept offering her cups of tea, or he saw to it the countess stayed on and married Reg. For the moment he chose the tea. "Sure you wouldn't care for a cup, miss?"

"It's Melissa, you know."

"The child calls you Miss."

"It's a nickname. She couldn't pronounce Melissa when she was two."

"It's personal, then. Miss."

Her eyes widened slightly. It wasn't a title anymore, it was a key, a way in.

She fidgeted. "I'm getting in your way."

"I'd never say that. Miss."

She frowned. Somehow they'd strayed from her carefully planned track.

"So you're against marrying," he said.

FIVE

"It's fine for some people," she replied. "I just don't believe it lasts."

Most people saw the sense in loving one person for life, Reilly thought. Most people dreamed about it. "My parents were married nearly forty years when Mum died."

"I'm sorry to hear that."

"It was a few years ago, Miss." He looked up when her silence continued.

He found her squinting at the ceiling. "Let's see. If they were married forty years, you must be somewhere around—"

"Thirty-six. The eldest of three sons."

"Ah."

"I hope you'll take no offense if I show less interest in learning your age. I've found women don't appreciate it."

She laughed, charmed by the hint of flirtation in his voice. Reilly never thought himself adept with women.

He'd play Mel Gibson himself if it made her smile. "What about your parents, then?"

"What about them?" she asked brightly.

"If you tell me how long they were married, I might guess your age."

The smile disappeared. "What does two years tell you?"

Reilly held her gaze when she would have averted it. "Broken home?"

"Unraveled is more like it. Dissolved." She shrugged and pushed off from the table. Unsure where to walk or what to do with her hands, she joined him at the sink, handing him plates, avoiding his look. "Love fades. Children don't. Even broken families can work, as long as children know there's someone who will always be there for them."

"Everyone needs that."

She shook her head. "Not me. I outgrew it. I learned not to wait for something that was never going to happen. I do fine on my own."

"With love to spare." She had so much love to give, and she gave it all to the child. "Is that why you became a nanny?"

Her smile immediately changed to a beaming grin. "The first day I met Aurora I knew I couldn't walk away."

Kind of the way Reilly felt the day he'd met Melissa. "What happens when she grows up?"

"You think I'm too attached?"

"I didn't say that, Miss."

"I know she'll go to school someday. She's smart as a whip. But Helene has to marry first, settle down."

"She might do that sooner than you think." If he had

any say in it, she'd marry Reggie tomorrow. "Your employer is rather single-minded."

"I think 'couple-minded' is more like it."

They shared another laugh. This time they welcomed the silence that followed. Reilly wondered whether Reg would buy the idea of eloping, say next week. "If I may venture an opinion, Miss—"

"What?" Her mouth dropped open. She propped one elbow on the counter, one hand on her canted hip. "As if you need my permission for anything. It's not as if *I'm* a countess. I'm a working stiff, like you." She playfully punched his arm.

Reilly played along. When she let down her guard, she was sassy and pert and as tart as the fresh-squeezed orange juice he prepared for Reggie every morning. He didn't mention he'd served two glasses to the master bedroom yesterday; he didn't want to shock her. Although the suggestive substitution of what she'd be like in his bed sent a throbbing ache through his lower body. Lord, he wanted her. For the time being, he chose to preserve the easy camaraderie they'd discovered. Moments such as this were as rare as answers to his erotic dreams.

"In my 'umble opinion," he repeated with a grin, "the more I see them together, the more I believe His Lordship would make a loving husband and a loving father. He seems genuinely fond of Aurora."

"You've been watching that too."

He'd known it was important to her. "It's a consideration. Besides the countess's feelings for His Lordship, that is, and their—what did you call it—commonality?"

A touch of color dotted her cheeks. She threw her

head back and laughed. She raised a glass in need of washing.

He picked up another, clinking it against hers.

"To a fine couple."

"Long may they reign."

He looked too long in her eyes. When she moved away, his heart clenched like a fist. He didn't want to lose the feeling. There was something wonderful about wanting a woman. Sharing was something he hadn't allowed himself in a long time. And this one—

This one traced a cut-glass goblet with her fingers while she considered her retreat.

"I'm sure His Lordship would look after the girl," he said, fumbling for something more.

She looked directly in his eyes, her voice surprisingly ardent. "*You'd* look after her, Reilly. If she lived here, I'm sure she'd be the safest, most-cared-for little girl in the whole world."

And her nanny? He wanted to care for her.

Her hand rested on his arm. Her fingertips touched his rolled-up sleeve, her thumb grazed the hair on his arm. Her gaze faltered when she realized she was touching him again.

"It's good of you to say so, Miss."

She huffed, glad of the excuse to withdraw. She gave him another sassy glare, repeating his words in a mock-Yorkshire accent. " 'Good of you to say so!' You're so formal."

"What else would you want me to be?"

She crossed her arms and planted both elbows on the counter's edge, her pert behind wagging in the air. "What do you do to relax around here, anyway?"

Being teased by a beautiful woman until his blood

hummed in his veins wasn't any man's idea of *relaxing*. He kept his eyes firmly on the sink.

"This?" She slapped the water, splashing suds, breaking up his reflection.

"I like knowing everything's in its place."

"Mm. Compared to bomb disposal, I suppose anything's soothing."

He grinned, unable to fathom why his heart pounded like a drum.

She'd sidled up beside him, her thigh glancing against his. "Okeydokey. If this is relaxing, what do you do for excitement around here?"

He kept his eyes off her for starters. His imagination provided all the excitement he could handle. His body took it a step farther. For once he was glad he'd worn his full-length apron. He worked his way down the counter, wiping it with a dishcloth.

"Excitement," he repeated, reaching past her to yank the chain on the stopper. Water whirlpooled down the drain.

"How does a vital, young, reasonably handsome man—"

"Thank you, Miss."

"You're welcome. You interrupted me."

"Sorry, Miss."

She chuckled. "How does such a man prevent himself from becoming as sedate, mannerly, and musty as this old house?"

"One finds few opportunities for excitement," he replied in measured tones.

"I should say not. Everything's under control. The gardens are trimmed and pruned. The horses are fed and bedded down. The other servants are asleep. . . ."

In other words, they were alone. Reilly concentrated so hard on the soapy water, one would have thought the Loch Ness monster lurked in its depths. He remembered everything he'd ever learned about self-control.

She took his hand in hers, joining their soapy palms. "It's okay, Reilly. We can flirt. We can laugh at it too. That's why I came down tonight. I thought if we could talk like two normal adults, we could put the rest of this behind us. You have to admit, it was getting a little ridiculous."

Him wanting her? Never. She gave his hand a motherly squeeze. It felt like an iron band tightening around his heart.

"We've gotten past whatever it was that was between us," she declared.

"Are you sure?"

"If we hadn't, I couldn't talk to you, tease you like this." A hip bump. "Chemistry, that's all it was. Sparks, looks, lust. Whatever arcs between men and women like static electricity. It's over and done, and I say good riddance." She slapped the counter. "We're much better off as friends. Don't you agree?"

He grunted. Turning on the faucet, he rinsed a goblet until it glittered. He held it like something precious and fragile, all the while clenching his jaw until a vein beat.

"I hope you don't think I'm being too forward," Melissa stammered.

"Never."

"We couldn't go on avoiding each other."

"No."

"Four days would be an eternity if we tried. Confront it and it'll go away, that's my philosophy."

So she wanted it to go away. He set the glass down so hard, it rang. Pulling the long apron over his head, he wadded it up and tossed it at a chair. He didn't even look to see where it landed.

Friendship, she said. She wanted something pale and pasty, as exciting as warm milk. "Do you know what I want?"

She gulped. Reilly *never* raised his voice. "A little peace and quiet? I can go."

"No." He took her face in his hands. Damp and moist, his palms smelled of soap. "I want you to stay."

"I, uh—"

"And don't say another word."

He pressed his body into hers, covering her shock-parted lips. The kiss didn't last long. Long and rangy, she nearly matched him in height, which excited him. So did her quickened breaths, the feel of her ribs expanding in the circle of his arms, her heart hammering in time to his—and the fact that she stayed.

He splayed his hands over her shoulder blades, pressing her forward. The small mounds of her breasts flattened against him. He breathed deep, his chest taut, his blood surging. He didn't want to stop. It was late, the house was quiet. A moan deep in a woman's throat, a series of ragged breaths wouldn't be overheard. They had time. Privacy.

She caught her breath. He stole it again. "I've wanted this from the day I saw you." He skittered his lips across hers, then opened her with his tongue. She groaned.

He loved the way she tasted. Her mouth was like satin, his tongue rasping across it. The musky scent of potpourri, smoke, and roses, wafted from her skin. "You smell like fireplaces and flowers."

"We shouldn't," she whispered.

"We shall."

"Reilly—"

"Hush." Another taste. Another lingering invasion.

Her body uncoiled against him. He urged her closer. She lifted slightly on her toes. The juncture of her thighs molded to the juncture of his. "Melissa."

The sound of her name opened her eyes. Where she stood, where her arms shamelessly gripped, the welcoming angle of her hips, shocked her. Doubt swirled in the depths of her blue eyes, drowning beneath the sensations they'd made together.

He said her name again, gruff, arguing, trying desperately to evoke a moment already slipping from his grasp. "Don't go."

She shook her head. "We're friends. We can't ask for anything more."

Maybe she couldn't. He was close to demanding it. Life was an all-or-nothing proposition. He'd settled for nothing for too long. A house wasn't a home; a job wasn't a life.

He dragged her back into his arms. He scraped his cheek's stubble along her neck, relishing her sharp intake of breath. That said it all, how right they were together, how simple it was, one body joined to another.

"This is crazy."

"This is real." It was the house that loomed like a fantasy around them, a dream of order and stateliness devoid of messy emotions and uncontrollable passions, free of the hate and anger that dogged him in Northern

Ireland. Empty of the love he thought he'd never need again.

The words poured out of him, unexpected, undeterrable. "There's a room in the east tower, a bath with a fireplace all its own. Tiles on the walls, candles on the hearth. No one can see in."

She hiccuped when he nipped her neck, breathlessly waiting for the next rush of words.

"I'd wash you there. I'd spread soap across you, your shoulders, your breasts. Between your legs—"

She shook her head, shuddering as his hands stroked her arms, the slope of her lower back. Fully clothed, she lived every sensation as he spoke it, trying in vain to deny him. "You're a sorcerer."

"Come with me."

"We can't."

"We can. We can go there. I can show you." He extended his hand toward the running faucet, interrupting the crystal rope of lukewarm water. He filled his palm and brought it to her mouth.

She glanced nervously at it, as if he expected her to lap at it. For a burning moment the idea made his pulse pound. He watched her pupils dilate.

He slid his cupped palm down the side of her neck, stroking her as water dribbled between his fingers. Her lids fluttered shut. Her whole body trembled. He tipped his hand. Water cascaded down the front of her blouse, trickling into the V, glistening on her flushed skin. Her mouth came open in a silent gasp.

He flattened his wet palm to the base of her throat, capturing her thudding pulse, moving ruthlessly downward.

A moan tore from that pale throat. "Don't."

"That's just a taste." Flesh against wet flesh, he spread his fingers inside her blouse, tugging until a buttonhole opened, then another. He cupped her small breast in his hand. The damp lace of her bra clung to her erect nipple.

She groaned.

No was only a word. He listened to her body. He spread the limp fabric of her blouse, dipping his head to lave the mound of her breast with his tongue. Her knees gave way. He caught her against his thighs, moving one leg between hers, feeling her sweet heat gathered there, smelling it—

"No!" She wrestled out of his grasp and staggered backward. The exit to the garden was closer than the staircase. She backed toward it. "This is not what I came for."

He stood alone at the sink, frustration darkening his features.

She clutched her blouse at the neck. "I came here offering you friendship. You misinterpreted what I—"

"Don't lie," he said, his voice burlap rough. "Not to either of us."

"I never meant—"

"You wanted that. You need it." He took one step toward her, saw her flinch, and took no more. "You need what I can give you. You need touching, loving, handling. A man who can fill your body with his, love you until you're weak. A man who will kiss you until the fire's so strong, you beg to have it quenched."

"You've never talked to me like this."

"I've wanted to."

The rawness in his voice stopped her breath. She saw now why he'd kept such distance. He'd known that any break in the facade, any crack, and these words would tumble out, rushing at her like a wall of water, a swelling tide. Behind that discreet facade a turbulent passionate man caged his feelings. Until she reached for the lock.

She shook her head. This was too much, all those tempestuous words and passionate promises. It was too much like love, like the absurd infatuations her mother got swept up in. She couldn't trust a love that exploded out of nowhere. It didn't happen that way. It didn't happen at all. "This isn't real. It's lust, it's loneliness. We hardly know each other."

"You need a man. Someone you can share some of that love with instead of wastin' it on a little girl."

That stung. She pulled her shoulders back. "You don't know what I want."

"Don't I? I've never met a woman as needy as you."

Like a splash of ice water, the words hit her. "I am not needy!"

He cocked one hip against the sink, measuring her from head to toe with a look. "You're a woman, aren't you?"

She felt dizzy, sick. Had she come across as that desperate? She clenched her fists at her sides. "I'll be gone in four days. Until that time, I'd appreciate it if you left me alone." She spun on her heel, slamming the door behind her.

Reilly shut off the faucet with a twist of his wrist. He waited while the jolted windowpanes rattled themselves silent. Then he stared at himself in the black window above the sink. He'd meant what he said. If she listened to her feelings instead of her fears, she'd know how right they were together. She belonged there, with him.

But who was he kidding? He'd made the wrong move

at the wrong time. And stood by helplessly while the whole sorry business blew up in his face. It wasn't the first time. "What do you do now, mate?"

The kitchen's hollow silence was his only answer.

The ragged stones of the archway felt good against Melissa's cheek. Their edges prickled against her palm. In a minute her heart would slow, her frantic emotions settle. Until then her stomach coiled and churned, her cheeks burning with humiliation. Goose bumps broke out over her skin. She welcomed them.

The water stopped running in the kitchen. She glanced at the door, suddenly afraid he'd follow. She fled into the garden, using the moon-cast shadows to guide her down the white paths toward the woods.

"How could you?" The question taunted her with every step. She drew in deep healing breaths. They didn't help. They brought the smells of smoke and roses to her nostrils, the scent of Reilly in her arms.

Fireplaces and flowers, his words for her scent. Hours before, she'd sat beside the fire in the library while Lord Darby read to Aurora. Listening to His Lordship's murmuring baritone, Helene beamed. Aurora cuddled. Melissa took a spot near the crackling flames and thought of Reilly. When the little girl had fallen asleep, Melissa had taken her upstairs. More eager than she'd wanted to admit, she'd put Aurora to bed then splashed her face with rose water and taken the backstairs to the kitchen, hoping to find him, hoping . . . For what?

I only wanted to talk to him, her mind insisted.

Her heart told another story. One that thrilled at the

idea of a man being so attuned to her body he tasted the smoke and roses on her skin. When he kissed her she crumbled in his arms like rose petals. Why? Why had she succumbed so fast?

His parting words cut deep as a knife. *You're a woman, aren't you?*

He'd called her needy. She repeated it as if it were the filthiest five-letter word in the language. Needy was what her mother was, what she'd vowed she'd never be. She'd never throw everything away for a man.

She'd come downstairs intent on putting things in perspective. Or so she'd told herself. She couldn't have been so blind to her own motives, could she? Her mother's mistakes weren't genetic, were they?

You're a woman, aren't you?

"Damn you, Reilly." She gritted her teeth and strode into the woods, branches snagging at her blouse, ferns slapping at her jeans. She was a woman and he was a very desirable man. She'd kissed him with everything she'd had, and he'd taken her actions to mean exactly what they'd meant. Need. Lust. Weakness. If he took her in his arms again, she'd probably do the same damn thing.

Footsteps thudded on the soft ground behind her. She ducked behind a tree.

A flashlight danced across the ferns as they wafted in her direction, whispering and pointing like traitors. "Melissa?"

She froze at the frustrated rasp of his voice.

"Melissa!" He sounded stern and strong, very male and very, very unhappy.

Let him croak her name. Hell would freeze over before she'd answer such a gruff summons. On the other hand, she sincerely longed to give him a piece of her mind. Needy, indeed!

He stopped ten feet away in the midnight gloom. The beam of light ceased its sweeping. "Go too far and you'll set off the security system," he warned her. "There are sensors every twenty feet. Break through one of them, and we'll have the constables here in five minutes."

He had a point. He also had a dog. Vandyke, one of Lord Darby's black Labradors, trotted happily from tree to tree. Far from sniffing her out, he seemed content to pad along beside Reilly.

She took comfort in his mute company. Anything was safer than being alone with Reilly. Her voice cool and composed, she called to him. "Over here."

Reilly swung around. The flashlight's beam began at her knees, climbing slowly. Her blouse was still wet. Damp patches emphasized her breasts' tight buds. She folded her arms and glared at the light.

He switched it off. "Will you come in with me?"

"I'd prefer some fresh air."

"I think I was fresh enough for both of us."

Her throat closed up. She didn't want him making jokes.

"You'll catch a chill."

"Whose fault is that?"

He snorted and stepped toward the sound of her voice. "Your teeth will be chatterin' in a minute. Take this."

He snapped the light back on. While the beam darted crazily over the trees he draped a coat around her shoulders.

"You think of everything."

His hands settled on her shoulders. "Just doing my job. Miss."

She closed her eyes, swaying into him. She braced herself for another kiss; a guilty corner of her soul longed for it. Instead she got what she'd asked for, distance. He withdrew his hands. It was the memory that weighed her down.

Shivering, she opened her eyes and pulled the coat's lapels closed. She was grateful when her voice emerged strong and smooth. "I'll have you know I am not needy, clingy, desperate, or any other spinsterish term you might find convenient when seducing female guests."

"You're not a guest."

"Then what am I?"

Reilly knew it as surely as he knew every inch of these woods. She was the woman he wanted. If he was going to keep her here, he'd have to go about this with a good deal more sense than he'd used up to now. "It's time we went in."

Stalking down the path illuminated by his torch, she blasted him with one accusation after another. He withstood them all.

"It's time I told you exactly where I stand. I don't believe in marriage. I don't believe in love. Your speech about baths and handling and all the rest of it was very pretty, but I *don't* believe in one-night stands."

"I was thinkin' of four nights."

She whirled on him.

Why didn't he simply hit the plunger and blow them all sky-high? He sighed and raised a hand, forestalling her next outburst. "I promise I'll not come near you for four days."

"Oh. Good." She turned and marched on until another thought stopped her dead in the path. "And the nights?"

He kept a grim smile to himself. "Nor the nights either."

"Marvelous." Chin in the air, she proceeded.

Reilly illuminated the start of the gravel path for her. Moonlight spread a translucent carpet of light along the ground. Gauzy beams tangled their fingers through her hair, a pale blue tint kissing her cheeks. Reilly directed the flashlight's beam straight ahead, climbing the back of her jeans, caressing them with a long shaft of light that settled between her thighs as she walked. Disgusted with himself, he switched it off with a click.

She jumped at the sound, moving a little faster.

Reilly wondered if the dark would make her skin taste any different, if her breasts would have the same sweet powdery taste her cheek had had, whether the shadows beneath her breasts harbored the musky aroma he'd inhaled beneath her ear.

He swallowed, contemplating four long days and four longer nights of torturing himself with memories. If he'd managed it differently, he could have led her to his bedroom. Maybe they wouldn't have gotten that far. He might have made love to her right in the kitchen, on the cold floor or the long oak table. Their bodies would have twisted and writhed, reflected in the copper pans overhead.

The fantasies got wilder as the house loomed closer. His dreams paled when up against reality. She'd said no, leaving him feeling like a fuse ready to blow.

But he wasn't working on his last job. Mistakes made here could be put right later. Sometimes life did give a man a second chance. He meant to make the most of his.

SIX

"Mummy invited us to dine with Lord Reggie tonight."

"It's Lord Darby, or Reggie, or sir."

"Or Papa?"

Melissa's smile froze. She didn't want Aurora getting her hopes up, especially since Helene had already asked her to pack. "We planned on leaving tomorrow you know."

"Maybe. Maybe not," the little girl singsonged. Her blue eyes twinkled as if she knew something her cautious nanny didn't.

"Just don't get your hopes up, puppet."

"I'm not."

"Then you're a better man than I, Gunga Din." Melissa tickled her until Aurora escaped to snatch a musty-smelling volume of Rudyard Kipling off the nursery shelf. Melissa wished escaping life was as easy as escaping into books.

As much as she tried to put Reilly out of her mind, he wouldn't go. She blamed the house. It reminded her of him, solid, reliable, all-encompassing. A home she'd dearly love to claim. Everything ran at his understated command, firmly under his hand. She knew the feel of those hands.

Aurora snuggled beside her on the window seat with her book. She flipped to the illustrations first. "I like your pictures better."

Melissa kissed the top of her head. "Thanks, puppet."

"Will you finish the picture you started of Bedford House?"

"Someday." When it didn't hurt to think of the nicest home she'd ever left behind, of the man she'd turned away.

She had only to think of the word *needy* to cool her longings. His remark about "wasting her love on a child" stung. She hugged Aurora close; loving children was never a waste. But maybe he had a point. A woman had more love in her than that, longings and dreams only a man could answer.

A knight in shining armor.

Her mother had dreamed of such a man to carry her into the sunset. But where Sally saw romance and chivalry Melissa saw a row of empty tin cans in the west wing. She saw Helene's bags packed and ready to go. What better example that love never lasted? A woman, even a needy one, would be wise to keep that in mind.

She held Aurora's hand as they entered the dining room that evening. Helene had loaned Melissa a beaded black dress for the occasion. The slope of the neckline bared one shoulder. The pleated skirt hugged her hips in tight folds, slanting to her ankles in a dazzling sweep.

She'd welcomed the formality of their last evening; it gave her a final chance to show Reilly she had everything under control. She was ready to leave. She'd had lots of practice.

Aurora got on her tiptoes to kiss Lord Darby's cheek. He patted her head with genuine fondness. Holding a narrow cigar, he looked downright debonair. Helene looked spectacular, her dark hair sweeping elegantly and simply to her milky shoulders. She practically glowed.

Melissa tried to be invisible, choosing a seat far down the table. Reilly would be in the room somewhere. She refused to search the shadows for him. Instead she recalled the cut crystal he'd held beneath the faucet the previous night. Droplets cascaded down its surface the way bathwater beaded on heated skin. She wanted to be like that glass, untouched, impermeable.

He stepped from the shadows to pull out her chair. She nodded politely and sat. If he'd been any kind of gentleman, he'd have found a substitute for this evening. But her body knew intimately how far from a gentleman he could be. His deference was only an act.

And hers? She pretended to be immune while every nerve reacted to his closeness.

He pushed her chair in, his fingertips skimming her bared arm. She caught her breath, knowing the touch was intentional. A tight knot formed in her chest. He performed the same duty for Aurora, the child grinning as he scooted her chair forward.

"Thank you, Reilly."

"You're welcome, lass."

"A glass of wine to begin?" Reggie suggested brightly from the head of the table.

Melissa noted his hand entwined with Helene's.

Don't hold too tight, she thought. Luggage waited upstairs. If she'd ever needed proof of how undependable love could be, this evening made her case. Did Reggie have any idea Helene planned to leave in the morning?

Instinctively, her eyes searched for Reilly. She pictured him serving dinner night after night as Lord Darby took his meals alone in this cavernous room. Her whole body ached with loneliness.

In the heavily shadowed candlelit room, she couldn't find him. Like any good butler, he had a way of erasing himself from a room while life went on around him. Only she knew how physically, vitally real he was, how his body throbbed for hers. No one else saw through him the way she did. No one else cared.

Did she? The question shook her.

Being wanted and being loved were not the same thing. Love was a dream, a fantasy some women indulged. The people they left behind paid the price, deserted confused lovers and lonely abandoned daughters. She suddenly wanted to warn Reilly, to tell him they'd be gone in the morning.

"Miss?"

She started.

His face remained impassive as he leaned over her shoulder. "Would you care for the meat or the fish?"

She stared up at him. Near her, the invisible cloak of propriety failed. She sensed the urgency coiled in his body. "The fish, please."

He set a portion on her plate with a silver server. "Cook is particularly proud of this dish."

A bone lodged in her throat although she hadn't taken a bite. "Everything has been splendid so far." She had to warn him, to see his reaction. Would he be hurt?

Relieved? How could she ask when she didn't understand her own feelings?

Not for the first time, she wondered at the way love made fools of women. She respected Reilly for keeping his distance these last few days. That didn't stop her blaming him for the same coolness. Now that their stay was almost over, she hated to leave. "Reilly. I—I just wanted to say our stay here has been—"

He grew very still.

She twisted the napkin in her lap. "Thank you for all you've done," she concluded lamely.

"I tried to do as you wished."

Her eyes darted to his. His look said it all; she hadn't been out of his thoughts for a moment.

Aurora wriggled on the other side of the table. Reilly raised the silver tray, his arm brushing Melissa's in silent farewell.

She ate her dinner without tasting it, sensing his eyes on her throughout the meal. She licked her lips, dabbing her mouth with her napkin, and felt his gaze devouring her. She wiped a faint gloss of lipstick from the edge of her wineglass and felt his lips beneath her fingers. She ran her finger around the rim and listened to the crystal sing.

He was at her shoulder. "Would madam care for anything else?"

She looked directly at him, her strained tone contradicting her whispered words. "Yes, damn you. What have you done to me? I wanted friendship. Companionship. You turned this into a question of . . . of—"

"Life and death?"

She smiled grimly. "Melodramatic but true." Tomorrow they'd return to their carefully circumscribed lives, living for others, pretending they were alive.

He cleared his throat, his voice resolutely low, his gaze on the table setting. "Would you care for another glass of wine?"

"Not wine." Another kiss. Another touch. Someone had to reach across the senseless chasm separating them. He was a man. She was a woman. If only they could keep love out of it.

He reached for her plate. She gripped his wrist with her hand. "Maybe I'm exactly what you say, I have needs. But don't you dare pretend you're more immune to this than I am."

His eyes lifted slowly to hers. "I believe I made myself clear, Miss. If you need me, I'll be there."

The remembered taste of his mouth filled hers, the press of his body branded her skin with new heat. "I didn't intend for that to happen."

"Some things are beyond our control."

"Maybe I was wrong to come to you in the first place."

"Is love ever wrong?"

The word fell between them like wax gliding down the side of a candle.

"Pardon me?" Reggie spoke up from the far end of the table. "Is there something wrong? Is the fish not to your liking?"

The first to regain his composure, Reilly replied. "A little more time might have made the difference, sir."

Reggie frowned. "Speak to Cook about it, will you? That's very strange. Very unlike her."

"I will, sir. Right away."

"And get the champagne, will you?"

Reilly disappeared through the hidden door that led to the kitchen. He reentered with a bottle of champagne, uncorking it in the corner. A chilled fog uncurled from its throat. He filled a set of fluted glasses, handing the first to His Lordship.

Reggie harrumphed and rose. "Ladies and—more ladies. Helene, my dear. Aurora, my little princess. And Melissa, wonderful efficient Melissa. It has been our great pleasure having you here. Believe me when I say Bedford House has seldom been graced by so many beautiful and charming women at one time. We've been honored."

"Here, here," Reilly murmured as he served a half-filled glass to Aurora. She giggled when the bubbles hit her nose.

Reilly brought the tray to Melissa. Since she was the last served, he lingered beside her. The thin and delicate glass trembled in her fingers.

Reggie delivered his speech with amazing smoothness and self-assurance. As if he were delighted, Melissa thought. As if he had no idea three bags waited upstairs.

He raised his glass to the ladies. "Am I the only gentlemen present to drink their health? Reilly. You, too, old man. Drink up."

Reilly filled a glass and raised it. "To the ladies."

At the sound of his gruff voice, Melissa's heart sank. She sensed his stormy eyes strafing her, willing her to look. Reggie's gaze rested on Helene in the same insatiable way.

"We've had a wonderful stay," Helene crooned. "I've loved every minute."

"Then may the next month be even more precious." Reggie covered her hand with his.

"I'm sure it shall be."

"My dear."

"Darling."

Melissa blinked. She wasn't sure what she was hearing. For his part, Reilly set the magnum in the ice bucket with a subdued rattle.

"We're staying!" Aurora announced.

"Yes, dear," her mother replied. "Reggie's asked us to spend all of June here. Would you like that?"

"Oh yes!" The little girl squirmed down from her chair before a startled Reilly could pull it out for her. Running to the head of the table, she threw her arms around Reggie's neck.

Melissa's stunned glance caught Reilly turning away. He hadn't known about this either.

Helene smiled blissfully. "Is anything wrong?"

"The packing," Melissa whispered between clenched teeth. "The bags."

Helene laughed indulgently, receiving Aurora's next hug. "Those are for Aurora and me. You didn't pack one for yourself, did you?"

"I assumed—"

"Reggie's invited us to London to see the apartment he uses when the House of Lords is in session. Isn't that right?" She extended her elegant hand.

Reggie seized it. "It's not much. A Georgian flat. Some antiques I've picked up here and there."

"You'll manage fine without us," Helene assured Melissa. "Aurora and Reggie and I will be a little family."

Reilly stepped forward. "Excuse me, sir, will you be requiring my services?"

"Nonsense," Reggie replied. "I think I can handle two days in the city. Pack a bag; I'll be fine."

They'd all be fine, Melissa thought, studying them as if from a great distance. Helene and Reggie could barely take their eyes from each other. Between them, Aurora looked positively ecstatic.

Her conscience told her it was wonderful news. Aurora needed to spend time with her mother, to feel wanted and included. But her heart wasn't buying. No matter how she told herself it wasn't the same, old sensations crowded in. Always a witness to other people's happiness, she watched as another newly formed family slowly squeezed her out.

Melissa saw Aurora and her mother off the next morning. Roaming the large house and its empty rooms, she seized on her painting kit. She would *not* feel sorry for herself, and she would *not* begrudge Aurora some long-needed attention from her mother. She'd do something she did well, losing herself in color and light.

Two hours later, on a hillside overlooking Bedford House, she surveyed the watercolor she'd painted the week before. Aurora would love it. It looked down from a meadow not far from the spot where they'd had their picnic that first day.

She threw herself into her work. She loved painting things her art professors would have sneered at, detailed depictions of castles they'd visited, valleys and waterfalls and landscapes. Along with them, she invented stories for Aurora, the kind Melissa had never heard as a girl, all dragons and princesses.

She chuckled as she dabbed her brush in a soft sky

blue. Words and pictures brought out a peacefulness in her that rivaled the manor house and grounds spread so graciously before her. "I wonder who enjoys my stories more—me, the child, or the child in me?"

"What about the woman in you?"

Reilly. She bit down on the brush she'd set between her teeth and took a deep breath. Better to face him, especially if they'd be working together for the next month. "You have a way of sneaking up on a person."

"Discretion is an art."

"You weren't so discreet the other night."

Reilly's voice grated. "I kept my distance, didn't I?"

She wondered. He hadn't approached her since that night in the kitchen. However, he'd stayed near in other ways. He'd poured her wine at dinner, watching her sip, swallow, lick a droplet from her lips. He'd ladled a creamy sauce over a delicately pink salmon fillet and handed it to her on a plate. He'd been completely proper and sinfully suggestive. No one had noticed a thing.

Except Melissa. Each time she tasted a spicy wine, she thought of him.

On the hillside her stomach growled. She flattened her hand over it. Reilly stood beside her as patient and unyielding as the house. Apparently he hadn't come here to make a move of any kind.

Melissa sat back on her camp stool and gestured at her easel. "All right. What do you think?"

"I can keep my opinion to myself. If it's unwelcome."

Convinced she'd gotten her reaction to him under control, she canted him a glance. "You've never done that before. For all your discretion, you manage to say exactly what you think." And *do* exactly what he wanted.

All the while he made her feel things she'd never dreamed, explicit wanton things.

He came closer. She sniffed his scent, woodsy and all male. He crouched beside her, studying the painting. "It's precise, Miss. But—"

"But?"

"Not quite real."

Relieved that he'd transferred his attention to the painting, she challenged him. "You're being tactful again."

He tilted his head and considered it some more. "It looks like a pop-up picture of a house in a children's book. Beautiful, exact, not something to live in."

"Then I captured it exactly." She brushed strokes of red on the chimney pots dotting the east wing, eminently pleased with herself.

"Bedford House isn't real?"

"It's a dream. They all are. Everywhere we travel—Paris, Salzburg, Venice—the hotels are first class and the houses opulent and luxurious. Helene was born to it, so was Aurora. But to me it's like living in a book or a movie." The dreamworld inhabited by the very rich only added to her feelings of never truly belonging. She let the thought come and go, dabbing at the tiles on the sloping roof of the conservatory.

Reilly sat down on the grass beside her stool, four or five feet away. Melissa studied him out of the corner of her eye. He wore wrinkled khaki slacks and a white cotton shirt. Sleeves rolled up, collar unbuttoned, he looked very rough-and-tumble, like a man who enjoyed hard physical work and didn't get enough of it. The memory of his fingers' light calluses came back to her. Her spine tingled. She dabbed at her painting.

He plucked a piece of grass to chew on, his wrists balanced on his upraised knees. Aware of her sidelong glances, he looked over. "What are ye thinking?"

"This is the first time I've been able to picture you as a soldier."

"Oh, aye. Not the usual kip."

"Pardon me?"

He cleaned up his accent, unconsciously straightening his posture as he did so. "Not in my usual uniform. I worked in the garage this morning. Did a stint of gardening after tea."

"You garden too?"

"Crowley lets me putter as long as I don't kill too many of his cabbages. Had me digging post holes till I noticed you sitting up here and snuck away."

"Nice to know at least one person on this estate bosses you around."

"Crowley's been here longer than any of 'em. Won't let me near the flowers, but he figures a strong back's gotta be good for something. A race of gardeners, the English are. Daft about plants."

"Aren't you English?"

"My father came from Ireland looking for work in the sixties. A lot of Irishmen did. Liverpool and Leeds are full of us. Manchester too. We're never considered entirely British, though."

"But you served in Northern Ireland," she said, treading on sensitive ground. "On the British side."

"I needed the job. I liked the idea of defusing things. Thought it might spread."

"It didn't work, huh?"

He noticed her looking at his face and fingered the scar. To her surprise, he laughed. "Don't go gettin' any grand ideas about my brave career. I got this the final week of basic training."

"You didn't!"

"Nighttime dash through an obstacle course. Got hung up in some razor wire I should've crawled under."

"Ouch."

His warm chuckle echoed over the hillside. "That's a brave lad, innit? You thought I got it doing something daring, then?"

She nodded sheepishly.

"I'll remember that next time I need to impress the ladies."

"And who might they be?" She went back to her painting, hoping to keep him talking by pretending his answers were simply conversation.

"The ladies in my life," he mused, tossing aside the blade of grass. He lay back, his hands behind his head.

His body was sturdy and thick, his muscles delineated by the cotton shirt. Melissa thought of the remote ideal he presented in his uniform, comparing it with the rugged man before her.

She'd already decided that his near-magical ability to reassure people sprang from his steady patience. She'd noted that the first time they'd met. But there was another reason people felt at ease with him. He conveyed a sense of knowing everything that went on around him, of seeing more than other people. She sensed him watching her, even though his eyes were trained on the sky.

At times like this, with him waiting patiently, she relaxed almost against her will. Sensing that he knew what she was going to say even before she said it, she was tempted to open up to him, to reveal things she kept to herself. She chose instead to ask about him. She needed to know more than the feel of his body or the sensations building in her own. She wiped off a brush. "What happened?"

Their eyes met. She didn't have to spell it out. For that they were both grateful.

"In Ulster?"

"Yes."

He thought before speaking. "I met a woman."

She put clouds in her sky.

He dragged a long slice of grass through his teeth, gnawing at the tip. "Her name was Clare, like the county. I met her in a pub. She had the kindness to come up and talk to me. Guess I was flattered to be singled out. We're not exactly welcome over there."

"She must have known what she was getting into."

"Aye. Me mates warned me away. I thought love would make a difference."

"She didn't hurt you, did she?"

"I hurt her."

Melissa set her brush down. "I don't believe that," she said softly.

He broke a piece of grass in two. "I knew enough to be discreet, visitin' her after dark, sneakin' out before the sun came up. Thought I was protecting her, slippin' out the widow's window at dawn."

"She was a widow?"

"Lost her man in a shoot-out in Derry. Moved to the countryside. She was lonely, that's why she fell for me. She needed someone, a bedmate, a man to take the sexual edge off."

Melissa colored. She returned to her painting, surrounding the house with splashes of deep green shadows.

Reilly continued. "I told myself it was more than sex, though everyone else told me otherwise. One day we got a phone call at the barracks, a bomb at a house. By the time I got to Clare's place, it was too late."

Melissa looked stricken.

He shook his head. "She got out in time. No one hurt. But her house was rubble, her new life up in smoke. She was in shock when I got there, screaming at me to go away, get out. Told me I was less than useless; which was true. Told me I didn't belong there and never would. That I was only good for one thing. So I was."

Another long silence enveloped them. The wind sighed over the hilltop. "I'd be obliged if you didn't say it," he added gruffly.

"Say what?"

"That it wasn't my fault. I didn't plant that bomb."

"You would have saved her house if you could."

"I shouldn't have started something I couldn't finish. I was building a house on sand."

Melissa gazed down on Bedford House. "Is that why you took up Lord Darby's offer?"

He propped himself on his elbow, nodding down the hill. "This is what I saw that first day when I hiked up from the village. It looked like a storybook to me too. I decided I'd stay here the rest of my life, if he'd let me."

It was a vision he'd needed, something timeless, stable, somewhere he could earn his right to belong. "You'll be caretaker more than anything," Reggie had said. The word appealed to Reilly. To take care. There was nothing he'd rather do, then or now. This woman needed care.

"You feel at home here?" she asked.

He looked up at her. "Aye."

"I envy you that. I'm always a guest in someone else's home, one of Helene's apartments, here. Starting anything with anyone is impossible," she concluded gently.

He'd had a lot nastier warnings than that. He'd laid his life on the line more than once, not knowing what the outcome would be. A steady hand and an uncluttered mind—that's all he needed. He wanted to make her part of the place he'd made his home. He needed her. And she needed him.

He thought it best not to use those precise words. Instead, he stood up, slapping the grass from his work pants. "Service doesn't hold the stigma here it does in your country. A man of my background and class wouldn't have many opportunities to run an operation as big as this. I oversee a staff of twenty-five, handle the budget, and tend the operations of the farm. I like the work and I'm good at it."

She squinted at a detail on her drawing, settling an unspoken issue with a bold stroke of blue. Unconsciously gnawing her lip, she tilted her head to the side. "Don't you ever get lonely in your perfect world?"

"I left you alone for four days, didn't I?"

A breeze slithered over her ankles. A chill wound up her spine. Melissa dabbed at her paint tray. "I meant for other women."

"There haven't been any others."

A group of colors ran together, hopelessly smudged. She cursed, dabbing at it with a tissue. He waited. "Last night I was sure we'd be leaving in the morning."

"We've got a month now."

"Unless Helene and Reggie argue. Then what? My life isn't entirely my own."

"You're lonely too."

"I have Aurora and don't you say a word against that." She stabbed her brush at him. A drop of paint flung off its tip. A blue dot landed on his slacks, an inch away from his zipper.

Melissa ducked her tissue into a bowl of water, reaching without thinking to dab at the stain. When she saw where she aimed, her elbow ricocheted right back to her side. "I'm sorry. Here."

He took the tissue from her, his crooked smile mocking her consternation. "I'll get it meself."

Blushing furiously, she bent to gather up the painting supplies scattered around her.

"You didn't let me finish," he said, referring to their conversation.

"Please. Don't let me stop you."

"I'm all for loving children. I'm also for lovin' women when they need it."

Needy again. She bristled. "I don't know if that's refreshingly frank or the most arrogant, self-impressed—"

He dropped the tissue and stepped closer, his body blocking the sun. Melissa looked up, her nose almost even with that blue dot.

"I'm sayin' it the only way I know how. I've been happy working for His Lordship. Until you got here, I didn't know what I was missing. Believe in it or not, you belong here every bit as much as I do."

"I'd know that better than you."

"Would you?"

Muttering about Neanderthal men, she scooted

around on her stool, snapping her paint case shut. "I think I liked you better as a butler, Reilly. Just because *you* need a woman—"

He plunged his hand into her hair. Instead of pulling her to him, his palm shaped to her scalp, delving beneath the surface, learning her in places she'd seldom been touched.

He pulled her so close, her chin nearly brushed the fabric of his slacks. He let her sense the tension in his body, the heat radiating from it. "I've always been willing to work for what I want. I'll work for you."

"What's that supposed to mean?"

"Your four days are up."

If only her voice weren't as breathy as the wind. "Don't I have a say in this?"

"You had your say. In my arms."

"It was a moment of weakness."

"A moment of truth."

He could have kissed her. He let go instead. Sauntering down the hill, he observed the ancient formalities of the duel. At ten paces, he stopped and turned. "I mean to have you, Melissa. I thought you should be warned."

SEVEN

To think she'd admired Reilly for his self-effacing tact! Beneath that detached exterior, that serene competence, the man had an ego bigger than the Isle of Man. Did he expect her to swoon with anticipation? To run away at the first sign of manly interest?

She had, hadn't she?

She winced, rationalizing like mad. His kiss in the kitchen had caught her off guard. His visit to her hillside had been equally mistimed. She'd allowed herself to gaze on Bedford House until looking became longing, yearning for a sense of permanence in her life. When he'd spoken of first arriving there, she'd envied him, torn by desires that were all mixed up. For him. For this place. For something she'd never had; someone to love her for herself alone.

Pacing her room that evening, she flipped through the watercolor sketches she'd made of the grounds so far. They were Aurora's pictures as much as hers. The thought anchored her. She'd never betray that fragile trust by rushing headlong into some hopeless love affair.

Leaving her latest sketch propped on its easel, she bundled the rest into her portfolio. Tying it shut, she quickly reduced the black string to a hopeless knot. "I swear, you taught Aurora to tie her shoes faster than this." Wrapping everything up in neat bows wasn't as easy as it looked. The symbolism made her scowl.

Yes, she had desires she denied. And yes, Reilly, with his supremely irritating aloofness and sudden heart-stunning intensity, had a talent for bringing them to a boil. Underneath, both of them were not the people they pretended to be on the surface. Was that hypocritical or simply human? Melissa wasn't sure.

Dissatisfied, she frowned at her last painting. It looked watery and incomplete. Her eye was drawn to squares of thick reds and deep greens, the sections she'd painted while he sat by her. The rest of the painting lacked their liveliness.

"Good thing Reilly isn't an art critic," she mumbled.

He detected in her needs she revealed to no one else. The brave way he proclaimed his wants shamed her by comparison. But she would never let him see how much she wanted him. Getting involved would only make it that much harder to leave.

Thanks to Reilly's cocky warning, her guard was back up—higher than a castle wall and wider than a moat. There were castle ruins south of Bedford House. She made herself a note to go looking for them tomorrow.

But first, she had a dinner date.

She appeared in the kitchen on the dot of seven. Imitating Helene's smooth self-assurance, she strolled toward the table, smiling politely as she braved the servants' startled looks. If she had to stay another thirty days, she'd show Reilly how easily she fit in. She was just another coworker. Surrounded by sensible, down-to-earth people, how could they be anything but?

Except that her senses went on red alert the moment she saw him. The twinkle in his eye told her he'd been waiting for her, expecting her. Like a distant star, the twinkle changed to a smoldering glow.

She nodded pleasantly at him. "Hello, everyone. Since we'll be working together for the next month, I thought it high time I stopped by."

"We're honored," he said. Carving a roast at the head of the table, he set down his knife, wiped his hands on a linen napkin, and approached her slowly.

Her heart did a little dance. Her smile remained fashion-model fixed.

Eyes questioning but demeanor unflappable, Reilly indicated the group. "You've met most of us in passing. Let me formally introduce you. This is Crowley, our gardener."

"Charmed."

The wizened old man ignored her outstretched hand. He touched his forehead as if tipping a cap. "Likewise, I'm sure."

Next came the security man, Haverford, and two under-housemaids, Cicely and Jenny. Barely out of their teens, they prodded each other and giggled as Melissa moved on to Martha, the upper housemaid.

"Skeleton staff tonight," Reilly commented. "Miller drove His Lordship to London and a few others have the evening off."

"We get tomorrow, though," one of the maids reminded him.

"I haven't forgotten."

Melissa wished she could forget the sensations warming inside her like embers every time Reilly rested his hand lightly on her back. It wasn't how he acted; it was what he knew, the secrets they'd shared, the intimacy.

She moved forward. The two girls watched them like hawks. The equally keen-eyed Cook, a plump woman of fifty, took Melissa's hands in hers, staring into her eyes as if they were tea leaves waiting to be read.

"You're that welcome," Cook said. "Let me get you an extra plate, love."

"Thank you very much."

"Are you comfortable, dear? Is the tea to your liking? I know Americans drink it differently than we do."

"It's wonderful. And I've enjoyed my stay immensely. I'm sorry I haven't met you all before now."

"You've had your hands full with the little one, haven't you?"

"I've chased her all over the house. Everything's so orderly, I sometimes get the feeling the place runs itself."

"Hardly," Cook exclaimed, laughing heartily. "A lot goes on behind the scenes the guests don't know about."

Reilly caught Melissa's eye. "Yes, it does."

Cook patted her hand. "We pride ourselves on that, love. Discretion, it's called. Every good house has it."

Reilly had it in spades. For all his passion in private, he'd never spoken to her in the presence of others without the utmost propriety. She felt his gaze on her at that moment, boring through her mercilessly, seeing her shaky performance for exactly what it was. She was denying her desires, papering over their true feelings with chitchat and social formalities. Much the way he did, Melissa thought, except Reilly was an expert at this, she a nervous amateur.

She took a seat at the end of the table while he took his at the head. Cook passed the vegetables. "This is such a fine house," Melissa stated.

Cook agreed. "A lot finer since our Reilly joined up."

"Oh aye, he's improved things one hundred percent," Martha declared.

"You wouldn't have recognized the place five years afore," Crowley added.

The staff recounted the sorry exploits of the last butler and the disrepair the estate had fallen into despite their best efforts. Next they launched into a critique of their present management, beginning with a round of good-natured grousing about Reilly's high standards.

Melissa noted the way everyone deferred to him. It was clear they respected him. And yet, no one got too close, no one trespassed across the invisible barriers he'd erected around himself.

No one but her.

He glanced up and caught her watching. Her gaze darted away, but not before her pulse sent a flare of color to her cheeks and a warm sensation curling down her spine. Patches of heat made her press her thighs together.

Reilly bit into a slice of rare roast beef, a satisfied smile creasing his face. Melissa turned as pink as the meat. How could she eat under these conditions? She'd never meant for this to turn into a scene from *Tom Jones*! She sighed with relief when the conversation turned to the countess. What was she like to work for? Was she fair? Appreciative? Did she believe in Christmas bonuses? Melissa laughed, fielding all inquiries.

An under-housemaid got straight to the point. "What happens if His Lordship marries your lady?"

Melissa paused, the idea hitting her full force. If Reggie and Helene married, she and Reilly would be around each other day after day, mornings, meals, meetings in hallways. Another kiss would be inevitable. And then?

"We won't know until that happens," Reilly murmured, filling in the silence for her.

Another maid took a new point of view. "And how would we manage if you married, Reilly? What if you upped and left us for some new mistress? What then, eh?"

"This blessed house is his mistress," Crowley grumbled.

Laughter drowned out Reilly's response. The maids exchanged knowing glances, tickled to catch their boss without one of his all-purpose replies. When the conversation returned to everyday matters, he caught Melissa's eye. There was no doubt who his intended mistress was.

"Is there too much curry in the soup?" Cook asked.

"It's fine," Melissa replied, her cheeks aflame.

The rest of the meal passed without further incident. Haverford drew Reilly into a low-spoken conversation filled with military acronyms and alarm codes. Crowley groused about messing up the property lines with wires and devices. The maids chatted about their plans for their day off. Cook moved on to pork seasonings she'd known and loved, her gaze only now and then darting from the butler to the nanny and back.

Melissa was too busy getting through this to notice.

She felt accepted. She felt vindicated. She'd shown him she could function in his world. And when the time came, whether next month or next year, she'd leave it without looking back.

Relieved to have spent one uneventful evening in Reilly's company, she chose the next morning to explore the woods, searching for the castle ruins that lay beyond the southern edge of the property.

With her camp stool in one hand and her paint kit strapped to a folding easel, she traipsed into the forest. Near the estate's perimeter, the trees grew denser and more tangled. She wrenched her easel from the arms of an interfering sapling.

Very well, she thought, if that's the way they wanted it, she'd sketch the gnarled old trees first. Aurora would like that as much as castles; princesses always got lost in magical forests.

She looked for a place to set up and paused. Through the trees the sun dappled a cottage's whitewashed walls with twisted shadows. Above it, moss grew brown and green over a thatched roof. She noted the tiny windows and their blue checkered curtains. Curious, thoroughly charmed, she let the picture take shape in her imagination. She'd make it a woodsman's cottage; a perfect place for a princess to hide from the wolf.

She never expected the wolf to step out and greet her.

She crossed the overgrown clearing, stepping over old leaves and mossy flagstones to get a closer look. Circling around, she found a door made of four dark green planks. The door swung open.

Melissa's heart skipped. Reilly stood very still.

He looked rugged and mussed, as he had the day before. His sandy hair was finger-combed, his cotton shirt unbuttoned at the collar. Had he been avoiding her? Or had he come to deal with the way she avoided him?

"I didn't know this was here," she said.

He took in her painting supplies with a glance, the stained oversized shirt she wore as a smock, the jeans and espadrilles. In the uneven sunlight, patches of shadow darkened his face. "Would you like to come in?"

If they were to be nothing but coworkers, Melissa decided this was the time to act like one. She stooped through the low door. Entering the cool interior, she laughed out loud at the sight. "Good heavens. It looks like Radio Shack!"

Twelve television monitors stacked three high and four wide along one wall. Video cameras in various states of repair littered a marred countertop. Wires, cables, rolls of electrical tape, and a computer covered all the other surfaces. Beyond a low archway she glimpsed a heating ring, a teakettle, and a pile of unwashed dishes. "I expected a charming little cottage, maybe a residence for Cook and Crowley."

"They prefer their apartment in the main house. This is the security hut. We monitor everything on the estate from here."

"Does Haverford live here?"

"He splits his duties between here and another estate. He's off today."

Reilly had given most of the staff the day off, she recalled. She briefly wondered if he'd done it deliberately. She nodded at the monitors. "It looks pretty elaborate."

If he sensed her nerves, he misinterpreted their cause. "It's precautionary. After the attempt on His Lordship's car, I thought it best. We're in no real danger."

Speak for yourself, Melissa thought wryly.

"It was the first thing I saw to when I got here," he added.

She scanned the rows of monitors. He was a man who watched over what he cared about. She felt his gaze on her. Unable to turn in any direction without sensing his alertness, she stepped further into the room.

She traced the worn oak floors with her toe. Despite the high-tech interior, the cottage was cozy. Massive age-darkened beams crossed the ceiling. An unused fireplace sat in a wall dividing the central room from the kitchen on one side and a bedroom on the other.

Her eyes strayed to the bed, unkempt, narrow. There was something lonely and unused about the place, separate, detached. Kind of like Reilly, she thought, observing, never participating, content to be on the outside looking in—until he got close to the woman he wanted.

And she turned him down.

"Wouldn't it be better closer to the house?" she asked, nodding toward the hardware. "Safer that way?"

"If the world was safe we wouldn't need all this."

And if a woman could love a man without fear of being hurt, they wouldn't need all this parrying.

Disturbed by her thoughts, Melissa studied the eerily silent television monitors. It wasn't Reilly she distrusted, it was love itself. Any woman would feel safe with him, cherished, protected.

The pictures switched every few seconds from the house's entrances to the stables, the gardens, the front gate. The garage was the only building with cameras on the inside. "The Rolls is gone."

"Miller took it into London for Lord Darby's use. They'll be back Monday."

"But they were due back tomorrow."

"I took the liberty of getting them tickets to a West End musical. *The Secret Garden*. I thought the little girl would like it."

Melissa forced a smile, determined to banish the idea he'd purposely won them even more time alone. The house seemed miles away. "That was very thoughtful of you, Reilly."

"Thank you. Miss."

She wondered what he meant when he called her that—a title to put distance between them or a nickname to erase it? She decided she didn't want to know. "Well, I should get started on my painting. You don't mind if I sketch it, do you?"

"You're an artist."

"My college major."

"Is that typical training for a nanny?"

She found herself eager to fill the room with absent people. "It was supposed to be a summer job. The day I met Aurora, that settled that. I knew where I was meant to be."

Reilly stepped between her and the door. "Did ye ever consider belonging here?"

"That's kind of a fanciful notion for such a practical man."

"I listen to my instincts."

She folded her arms, ready at last to take him on. "I have my priorities too. Aurora—"

"I'd never begrudge a child attention. I know she matters to you."

"She needs me."

"What do you need?"

"To get on with my sketching."

He snorted. "Women need loving too."

"Of a different sort than children, I'm sure." She tossed back an unruly strand of curls. "I got this part yesterday, Reilly. You flat out warned me, remember?"

"What's standing in your way?"

"You are. Now, if you'll excuse me."

"Are you afraid of being hurt?"

The man was like a rock. When he didn't want to move, he would not be moved. "Reilly, there's nothing we can do in one month together. That's if Helene doesn't get into a snit and order us all back to Paris tomorrow."

"Is she the type?"

The question made Melissa pause. Helene hadn't resorted to her spoiled socialite persona since they'd arrived. She relaxed around Reggie, utilizing all her polish and poise without the old pettiness rearing its head. She seemed *happy*.

Nevertheless. "Helene and Reggie have nothing to do with us. We couldn't establish any kind of relationship in a month."

"They have."

"It won't last."

"You can do it in a day, an hour. If you let it happen. Sometimes all it takes is a look." He touched her cheek.

She swallowed thickly. She'd meant to walk out of

there, head high, shoulders back. Then he touched her as if she were some cherished object. "Don't talk that way."

"What way?"

"Like a romantic."

"You don't believe it."

She shook her head, calling into service her most disdainful smile.

"Who was he? The man who hurt you?"

"There wasn't one. I never let one get close enough." She'd meant it as a warning, not a confession. She'd seen the men her mother hurt or the ones who hurt her. Love wasn't to be trusted in any form. Passion, that's all it was. Fleeting and ephemeral.

"I'd never hurt thee," Reilly said, lapsing into his Yorkshire accent. He dropped his proper accent around her, letting her see the man he was underneath. "I'd never lie to thee."

"It's myself I don't want to lie to. I don't want to start believing in fantasies."

"Is this fantasy?" The back of his hand skimmed her breast.

The breath froze in her lungs, filling them with a hollow ache. "Women lie to themselves about love. How important it is. How we can't live without it. We build expectations nothing can live up to."

"You don't."

"Love fools people, it fades. It's like the flu; people get over it."

He smiled because she was trying so hard to. His patient eyes hadn't released her yet. He slid the back of his hand up the side of her throat.

"Don't do this."

"I want thee."

"I'll leave."

"You can stay."

"It won't work."

"If you don't want to believe, I won't ask it of you. Just know this, I'm at your service. Night and day. Whenever you want. Whatever you want."

"Stop touching me," she commanded breathlessly.

He shook his head, a glimmer of a smile on his lips. "That's the one thing I can't do."

"I thought the wonderful Reilly could do anything."

He wanted to make her believe in love. He hadn't accomplished that. A week hadn't done it. A month might not. Maybe an hour could.

He opened his hand, running his fingertips over her cotton smock. Love consisted of a lot of things. She didn't believe in many of them. She didn't trust gentle. Affection scared the life out of her. As for sharing, she hadn't told him much about her previous life.

Whispering his fingers down her neck, he felt her distance, saw her mouth set. He displaced a strand of hair captured by her lashes and watched her eyes widen in dismay. She pleaded silently with him to stop. Not from fear but because he was reaching her. He kept on.

Sex wasn't usually the way to begin a relationship, but if he could get her to believe in this, to see the real physical side of love, he'd be one step closer to making her believe in the rest of it. By the time she realized all that went into loving a woman, there'd be no question in her mind that he cared for her.

He touched his lips to hers.

She trembled, melting by degrees.

"That's it, lass."

Her lids fluttered shut. He folded her in his arms. Soft and wet, the kiss went on for minutes. He said what he could—silently. She could forget her fears with him, he'd be there. She could be wild, shy, demanding or giving, he didn't care. He wanted to be there, to take her with him to someplace only they would have together, the space love made in two people's lives.

Melissa pulled back, catching her breath. "You agree with me, then. This can't last."

He agreed. Maybe somewhere down the line she'd notice that agreeing with everything a woman said was another way of loving her. He kissed her again.

He pulled her nearer, thrusting deeper. His tongue dodged and darted with hers, toying, cajoling, eliciting a fleeting smile and a heart-melting mew of pleasure. She said his name. He raked her neck with a bite that made her shudder. It could get rough. He wondered if she minded.

Inch by inch he felt her sink into him, two bodies forming one. Taut and thrumming, his flesh heated, a hard shaft unapologetically thrust between them. When he covered her breast with his palm, it was his hand that shook.

Hers were silky soft and steady, vining around his neck. "You were right. In the kitchen, I mean. I do need you. It's been so long."

The bare admission rocked him to his soul. He teased a nipple taut, her body bucking with tiny tremors. "How long has it been?" he asked, his voice tenderly gruff.

"Too long."

He put his desire on hold, treasuring her confidences

as thoroughly as her body. "Tell me about your last man."

"There haven't been many."

"I pictured 'em lining up for you."

She laughed, thanking him with a shy glance for his compliment. "In college I expected my boyfriends to graduate and go on to other things. And they did."

He hated that careless shrug, really he did.

"I knew better than to fall in love. Even then." The longer she thought, the more memories clouded her eyes. "Sometimes I wonder if I pushed them away."

She'd never do that to him. He unconsciously held her tighter, his tension a stark contrast to her languid undulations.

She sashayed softly against him. Eyes at half-mast, she studied his troubled look. She skimmed her fingers over his lips like a person reading braille. "Why are you doing this, Reilly? If I didn't know you, I'd think you were seducing me."

That was his secret. Torture squads couldn't force it out of him. He leaned forward to kiss her.

Her head darted back, a smile dancing across her lips. They might stand thigh to thigh, but her sweet mouth wasn't through with him yet. "You don't believe all that nonsense about love, do you?"

"No," he croaked.

She weighed that solemnly. "An affair is all we can have."

The lies backed up in his throat. He told her as much of the truth as she'd accept. "You're a beautiful woman. I want you."

"Do you?"

More than all the world.

She nuzzled his neck with her nose. "You want me?" she asked playfully.

He'd wanted her from the first day he saw her outside the helicopter, sick with fear and strong with courage. The spirited, confident, generous woman he glimpsed with Aurora and the cautious, vulnerable woman he'd seen in private—he wanted both of them.

He realized she was waiting for his answer. He cleared the gravel out of his throat. "I've never wanted anything more."

Too urgent. She scolded him with a look. "Just don't tell me it's forever."

If it wasn't, the memories would be. He'd make sure of that.

He curved his fingers into her collar, pulling the oversized smock off her shoulder, kissing the bare skin, drawing the sweet heathery scent of her into his lungs. "If sex is what you want, it's what we'll have."

"Good." She stared at his shirt, splaying her hands over his chest. Her eyes didn't meet his. "I won't let you down." She pierced him with a smile. "When it's over, I'll leave. I won't cling. I won't cry. I'll take my memories and be on my way." She tossed her hair again, light-hearted and gay—if a man didn't look too close.

He tugged her close, tucking her cheek against his shoulder. He had to resist the urge to shake her. A woman shouldn't settle for what little he'd offered. She should be making demands, extracting promises, putting her damn fool foot down. Instead she let him build this house of cards, lie upon lie, false promise after false promise. The only truth was in the thudding of their heartbeats, the way she smelled, the way he held her, and the taste of her in his mouth.

"You've been awfully good to me, Reilly."

"I try, Miss."

To his immense relief, she actually laughed. To his distress, she brushed her breasts against his chest and nuzzled his cheek with her nose. "You're a good man. Even when you are playing the world's stuffiest butler."

Stuffy, that's what the room was. He pressed her back toward the bedroom and left her standing in the doorway. He leaned across the bed to yank open the small window. The swollen wood screeched. A bird on the sill shrieked and flew off. The curtains fluttered. Reilly turned.

The bird wasn't the only one about to take flight. Melissa waited on the threshold, coiling a strand of hair around her finger. Reilly purposely eased the frown creasing his brow. He promised himself he'd take this slow, knowing the urgency in his veins would fight him every step of the way.

He reached for her, and she took a step forward. It was all he needed to undo the buttons on her smock. He opened it as he went, revealing her bare shoulders, the tank top she wore as an undershirt. While she fumbled with the rest of the buttons, he took off his own shirt, pulling it over his head. In that second of blindness the smock fell. Reilly held his breath at the sight.

Her tank top was ribbed, clingy, see-through. It held her breasts in its softly elastic grip, the taut nubs of her nipples pebbled with desire, straining against the cloth.

He kissed her collarbone, her shoulder, laving her precious skin with his tongue, finding her at last through the fabric. His hands roamed everywhere. He couldn't look her in the eye, not without lying again. He'd show her his love instead. He loved the scent of excitement coming off her, the feel of her breath on his cheek, the heat they made together. He'd use everything but words to tell her.

He'd even use the clumsiness of two people stepping out of their jeans, stretching out their hands to balance against each other. When she stumbled, he caught her in his arms. He laid her back on the bed in one move, aligning their bodies.

"I've dreamed about this," she whispered.

It wasn't a dream. He ran his hand down her thighs to show her, arguing a scrap of silk off her hips, revealing a triangle of red hair. "Tell me that isn't real."

She laughed softly.

He kissed her there and she held her breath. He tasted her everywhere, her belly, her breasts, stopping only when he reached her throat. "Tell me this isn't real."

She couldn't speak. With his lips on her pulse, his fingers parted her. She tried to turn her face; he wouldn't let her. He kissed her with his eyes open, watching her lids tremble, feeling her body do the same. He cleaved her again, her body satiny and slick around his fingers. She begged for more, a rising inarticulate cry cut in half by a captured breath, released by a low moan. "Reilly."

He wouldn't stop, not until he'd said everything he wanted to say to her, with his hands, his mouth, and his body. With love.

With everything but words.

EIGHT

The fireplace gave off an acrid odor of cold stone and black tar. He pulled up a chair and sat there, mocking his dour mood with visions of a crackling fire, a cozy room, a woman lying on a rumpled bed waiting for him to come back and finish.

He'd left her naked and quivering. The final after-shocks caused by his mouth and hands shuddered through her in spasms. He'd done everything he could, short of loving her. He'd told her this time was for her. Another lie. In real life he'd see to it she came first every time. He'd live his life for her if she'd let him.

Prudently, cruelly, he'd kept his mouth shut, telling himself he'd never win her love by declaring his own. So why did he feel like such a heartless bastard?

Crumpling a fistful of old newspaper, he tossed it on the grate then tumbled a log on top of it. He scraped a match to life with his thumb and watched the fire catch.

He'd given her as much as he dared, letting her take all she needed. When the pressure in his chest got to be too much, when words nearly overwhelmed him, when the truth grabbed him by the scruff of the neck and shouted that he loved her—he saw to it she finished as fast as possible. Then he got up and left.

Pants on, shirt slung over his shoulders, he sat in front of the flickering fire. He clutched a cup of tepid tea in both fists. Gulping it down, he hoped to God the sniffling he heard in the other room was due to the cold and nothing he'd done.

Or hadn't done.

A damp piece of bark spit out an ember. He knew exactly how it felt.

After a few minutes she glided into the room. She'd thrown on the oversized shirt she wore as a smock. The hem wafted around her bare thighs, teasing the rangy legs he'd coaxed around his body moments earlier, kissing her as intimately as he'd ever kissed a woman.

She hesitated on the cold floor then stepped nearer.

He couldn't meet her eye. Anger coiled inside him like wires stuffed in a fuse box. He didn't like shams. He didn't like using her to make a point. Even if the point was that he loved her, body *and* soul.

"Are you coming back in?"

The courage a woman had to have, he thought blackly. No wonder they ran from love. "I don't sneak out windows anymore."

"What do you mean?"

The fire sputtered; it wasn't working. Instead of catching, it kept threatening to go out altogether.

He'd never wanted to stop kissing her, to get the taste of her out of his mouth. He washed the anger out of his voice with another swig of tea. "I'd make love to Clare, be out the window, down the lane, and back in the barracks before dawn. My mates thought it was great fun, seein' me scamper about. When everything fell apart I told myself I'd never do it again. I'd never love a woman who didn't belong to me, in a place I didn't belong."

She padded around behind him, her hand coming to rest on his shoulder. "You belong here."

"I know." He leaned forward abruptly, stirring the cold ashes, trying to keep the flames alive. Her hand wasn't there when he sat back. "Now I need to find the woman."

If that hurt, she didn't show it. "There's no telling what will happen with Reggie and Helene. Until we know, there's nothing we can do."

He let the silence hang. Was what they'd just done nothing to her? She couldn't be his—she'd said so.

"Is that why you left?" she asked softly. She meant their bed.

"If I'm going to sleep with a woman, I want to sleep in her bed, wake up in her arms, call her mine and know it's true. I want to trust that it'll last. You don't want that. Do you?" He shot her a glance.

She looked as disappointed as he felt. "We agreed."

"So we did." Who was he to think he'd change her mind in an hour? He was bullheaded, stubborn, heartless.

"I should get dressed."

"Were you satisfied?" His curt question stopped her halfway to the bedroom.

A trace of sadness hovered beneath her smile. "You were very kind."

He reserved a brutal laugh for himself. "Then you don't know me very well."

He sensed her hesitate in the doorway, waiting for

something more, reassurance, concern, the kind of comfort a man gave a woman the first time he made love to her. Reilly knew exactly how it was supposed to be. Just as surely as he knew she'd throw it all back in his face if he tried to tell her he loved her. Who was the villain anyway?

After a minute she closed the bedroom door behind her. Why? he wondered. He'd seen the splash of freckles on her breasts, the long sweep of her waist, the downy blond hair on her legs, and the shock of orange red in between. She'd accepted everything he gave her—as long as he pretended it was only sex. Why act hurt now?

Because she's a woman, you twit.

He spat out a curse. He should never have played by her rules. He should have followed his instincts, loved her the way she was meant to be loved.

With a flick of his wrist, he splashed what was left of his tea on the struggling flames. Everything he'd worked for disappeared up the chimney in a puff of dirty gray smoke.

Melissa lay back in the bath. Striding from the cottage, she'd come in through the kitchen, telling Cook she wouldn't be at dinner that night. Then she'd fled to her room, too restless to sit, too confused to stay in one place. Gathering her robe and a few extra things, she'd gone searching, exploring the way Aurora did. She found the legendary bathroom Reilly had told her about, the one with the fireplace and tiles on the walls the color of the Mediterranean in July.

She'd tossed her towel down like a gauntlet, turning on the taps full force in the claw-footed tub. She congratulated herself on the sophisticated way she'd handled herself earlier. She'd said all the right things. No strings. No promises. No clinging. Things couldn't have been better.

Standing in the shadowy clearing outside the cottage, faltering for only a moment, he'd handed her her painting supplies. "You know your way back?" he'd asked.

A voice whispered in her heart: There was no going back now. She'd nodded and headed back to the house.

Seven hours later she relaxed into the steaming water. She poured a bottle of milky, fragrant oils into it.

"Wonderful," she murmured. Through slitted eyes she glanced at the deep blue tiles, their shiny undulating surfaces glistening and coated with steam. Her body shimmered the way they had as the water touched it, soothed it. Her skin felt tender, violated, stimulated. Satiny lotions caressed her everywhere. Slippery oils revived memories instead of washing them away.

She tied her hair in a ribbon and fluffed a towel behind her head. When she lay back, the ponytail formed a bump in the middle of her makeshift pillow. She grunted and retied her hair lower on her neck. The ends dipped in the water, so she flicked them over the tub's rounded lip. A draft whispered down the back of her neck. She grimaced and refluffed the towel, sinking to her chin in the water. So soothing, so comfy—

Who the hell was she kidding? A gallon of rose scents couldn't relax her. Every time she closed her eyes she felt him kissing her, caressing her, taking liberties that should have shocked her and had, heart deep, soul deep. Most shocking of all had been her response, welcoming him, opening to him as if they'd been lovers forever. As if everything she had she gave to him.

And she had.

Not that he needed to know that. When she'd stepped outside afterward, she'd searched for the perfect thing to say, something witty and cavalier. Something to let him know she hadn't taken this too much to heart. Helene would have found the perfect phrase. Melissa never was and never would be Helene.

She opened her eyes, glaring at the long narrow toes she'd never liked, wondering what he'd thought of them. Were her legs too skinny? Her hips too narrow? Had he been disappointed? Is that why he'd been so cool to her afterward? In the naked afternoon sunlight, he'd certainly seen everything.

Some women might have objected to the ambience, the gritty technologically sterile environment. Not her. Far be it from her to insist on something as transitory and ephemeral as romance.

She sat up, lurching over the side of the tub, flattening one breast to the cold porcelain as she reached for the washcloth. Scrubbing up a handful of suds, she started with her face, her arms, the smudges on her hands from wadding up newspapers to start the miserable excuse for a fire sputtering in the grate to her left.

What happened happened. She was an adult. She knew how flimsy love could be and how brief.

If only this one had lasted a little longer.

She hushed her heart, dragging her fingernails back and forth over the soap bar as if it were an emery board. "You're not going to do this. You are not going to second-guess it, rethink it, critique it, or blame either one of us." She dropped the soap like a depth charge and sank back to her chin. "A moment of pure chemistry, that's all it was. Lust is not romance. Romance is not romance."

He could have been a little kinder, not have left her there in the bedroom.

"And who told him I was fine? I like being alone?"

Nevertheless, she had every right to feel humiliated, spurned, indignant. In fact, she worked very hard to dredge up those feelings. A cool cleansing anger would be extremely refreshing.

The emotions withered as fast as she named them. She stared morosely at the tiny fire, mocking her with its crackle. Empty was the only thing she really felt. As if they'd lost something she hadn't even known they'd had, something fragile and irreplaceable.

She couldn't possibly love him. She was terrified of loving him. Loving meant losing, always. "What if I've lost him already?"

She squeezed her eyes shut. Hearts were like glass. Handing them to others entailed risk. But hugging them too close, holding them too tight, was no guarantee of their safety. They cracked all the same. It was obvious why Reilly turned her away; she'd let him body-close, but she'd never let him near. Inadvertently, unintentionally, she'd hurt *him*.

And she loved him too much to hurt him again.

She lay back in the water and groaned. The next time she saw him she'd make sure they both knew where they stood. Today had been an aberration, a onetime escape into a world that could never be. She was sorry if she'd hurt him, truly sorry. Leading him on would be unforgivable.

The fire popped. Outside, a board creaked. She opened her eyes. Reilly opened the door.

Sunk to her chin, Melissa clutched the sides of the tub. "Pardon me if I don't sit up."

He barely acknowledged her. With an armload of towels and a box of stout white candles, he made his way to the washstand. "This room is seldom used. I thought madam would appreciate extra towels."

She'd *ma*dam him. Let him adopt that irritating aloofness and pretend nothing had happened between them. She wasn't about to talk him out of it. This would be easier on him if *he* was the one who made the break.

She eased her grip on the tub, letting her shoulders relax. The water was murky with oils, too milky for him to see anything. Especially when he never looked. He ignored her as only a butler could, placing the towels in the cupboard, stocking the fireplace with kindling. "Would you care for another log on the fire?"

She shot him a smoldering look, anger suddenly flaring through her. "More heat would be wonderful."

He straightened his shoulders as if a knife had landed smack in the middle of his back. "Very good, Miss."

"I didn't expect you here," she said, chin tilted upward.

"I was in the garden. I saw the tower light."

She pictured him wandering the garden at this hour. She could smell the night air clinging to him, the herbal scents. In the humid closeness of the bathroom, she detected the familiar aroma of his skin. Memories cascaded through her. Beneath the water, she pressed her thighs together.

His voice sounded gravel rough. "The staff are off for the night. I wouldn't have come if it weren't discreet."

"I never expected less." She wouldn't ask for more.

"You didn't come to dinner."

"Cook sent up a sandwich." It remained on her bedside table. She had no appetite.

To her surprise, he pinched the creases in his slacks and sat on the raised hearth. Elbows on his knees, he studied her. "I should have said more."

Her heart gave a little dip. "Don't apologize."

"I hurt you. I promised I never would."

And I'm afraid I love you, she thought. *And I promised I never would.*

She cleared her throat. "You don't have to say anything, Reilly. This was never supposed to be about love. I didn't plan what happened."

"Are we going to pretend it didn't?"

She couldn't, nor would she ever forget it. "It was physical."

"That it was."

Beneath the water's surface, her toes found the slippery bar of soap and clenched it. "This isn't that large a house."

"I know who's in what part of it and when. And when the cottage is free."

He was proposing they meet again.

"I can be discreet," he added tightly.

"Don't be with me," she wanted to shout. She hated the way he wrapped himself in decorum and reserve. The way he held himself back from everyone, including her. Most of all she hated the fact that she'd made him do it, made it a prerequisite of their relationship that he speak no frothy words or promise her forever vows. "Maybe we should end this right here."

"It's just beginning."

"We got carried away, Reilly."

"We've done that before."

"Farther away."

"Over the moon."

She glared at him, color staining her cheeks. "You don't have to use tact on me; you weren't any happier with it than I was."

"It could have been better."

The humiliation she'd been courting all evening flooded through her. "Care to be more frank?"

As she grappled with the soap, it jumped from her hands. Reilly handed it to her, grazing her fingers with his. "Would you undo it if you could?"

She folded her arms over her middle. Her upraised knees were two bumps in the water, deserted islands in a white lagoon. "No, I wouldn't."

"I would."

She shot him a startled glance.

"In my old line of work a man didn't get second chances. I'd like another with you."

In the small room she could almost reach out and touch him. She kept her hands clamped to her body. "You don't mean that."

"I lied today."

She didn't want to hear it. He'd ravished her tenderly, passionately. No man had ever held her that way, focusing all his attention on her, anticipating every reaction. It frightened her how closely he listened to her rapid breaths, how thoroughly he knew her.

He'd lied.

"I don't believe it," she said.

"I love you. I pretended I didn't. We can go on pretending or we can be honest."

Her breath stopped. The room grew chilly, as if

someone had thrown open the tower window. She stood in a rush of water, rivulets sluicing down her body. She didn't care what he saw—he'd seen it before. She wanted one of those towels.

He stood to retrieve one even before she asked.

"You have no business loving me, Reilly."

"My business is seeing to it people have what they need."

"Then give me that towel. Please." Raised above him by the tub's height, she towered over him imperiously, a flashing-eyed redhead with a soaked green ribbon sticking to her chest.

He held it just out of her reach.

"I said give me that towel."

The woman was in no mood for dillydallying. She got hold of one end and yanked. In the oil-slicked tub her feet nearly flew out from under her. She screeched. He caught her in his arms. Her hips pressed flat against his chest, her nest of hair soaking his vest front.

She wrestled undeterred. "Let me go."

"You're on very slippery ground."

"Let me go."

"Not until I know you're safe."

She stopped wriggling. He repaid her reluctant obedience by dropping the towel at his feet. Then he placed his coat on a chair, calmly rolling up his sleeves. Three neat turns bared his left forearm. "It occurs to me you probably bathed Aurora when she was younger," he mused.

"What of it?"

"While I've never bathed children, Miss, it has been my honor to bathe Vandyke on those rare occasions when he tangles with a local skunk. He's also been known to roll in things. As dogs do."

She scowled, inching her way toward the washstand. "I don't see what any of that has to do with me."

Reilly finished the same three folds on his right sleeve, suavely stepping between Melissa and her goal. "What I mean, Miss, is that I've had some experience keeping unwilling participants in tubs. We're not done yet."

She practically crouched in the safety of the water. "You don't mean that."

He shoved his sleeves over his elbows. "Every word."

"You are not going to give me a bath." She slapped his hands away, arms flailing as she nearly lost her balance. "Stay away from me or I'll scream."

"We're in the east tower. No one will hear."

"You're a fiend. A monster. Who ever put you in charge of this house?" Her accusations would have carried a lot more weight if they'd been delivered by someone other than a naked woman dancing around a claw-footed tub, evading the ever-nearing Reilly.

He circled like a shark. "I said I loved you."

"And I said I want out of here. I warn you, I'll be out that door in a minute, towel or no towel!"

Slippery women in antique tubs made very unconvincing threats. Reilly merely stepped to the door and locked it with his skeleton key. He dropped the offending piece of metal in his vest pocket. As if reminded he still wore it, he unbuttoned the vest, draping it over the same cane chair that held a scrap of her underwear and her satin wrapper.

He stepped toward her. "You can make this easy or you can make it hard. Or should I say difficult?"

She glowered at him, his suggestive comment preventing her from lowering her eyes any further than his chin. She plopped down, taking grim satisfaction in the water sloshing over the edges of the tub. "I hope it ruins your shoes."

"I polish them every night."

He probably did, she muttered, lovingly buffing them the way he rubbed that bar of soap across the cloth. He knelt beside the tub, cupping her shoulder in his hand.

"What are you grinning at?" she snapped.

"I like washing up at the end of the day. I find it soothing, don't you?" Another handful of suds. Skin like satin.

"Being held against my will in a drafty tower room by a sex-mad butler is not my idea of a romantic evening."

He chuckled.

She held firm. She would not be charmed by clichéd devices like crackling fireplaces, the homey scent of fresh towels, the waxy aroma of candles, the swelling strains of Debussy on the radio, or the sinfully tranquilizing kneading of a man's hands. Being bathed was sensual heaven. He spread suds down her throat, rinsing her with the tilted palm of his hand. She remembered. The nap of the washcloth reminded her of a cat's raspy tongue. In minutes her weak-willed body had become indistinguishable from the water, floating, evaporating. Her eyes drifted shut. Might as well take losing with good grace.

His fingers found the last remaining tension in her neck. She muttered something about screaming; it was her last hope.

"If anyone could hear you from here, the legend wouldn't exist," he replied reasonably.

"What legend?" she asked, a million miles away.

"The legend of the third Lord Darby's unfortunate wife, the Lady Anne."

"Did he lather her to death?" That didn't come out right. Melissa was too tired to care. It had been a very long day. Emotionally exhausting. Physically draining. She didn't want to think about it. If she did, she'd have to acknowledge what his hands were doing to her.

Using her body's buoyancy, he lifted her out of the water with one hand. Her nipples were smooth brown aureoles, their centers barely peaked. The layer of suds he spread across them popped and tingled, each infinitesimal sensation producing a matching tingle deep inside her. And yet she felt no urgency. A ripple of warm water washed them away. Then another. Then the rasp of a cloth that wasn't a cloth at all but a man's tongue.

He lifted his face inches from her breast. Her skin pebbled as his breath feathered across it. He let her slip back into the water. "You bruise easily." When she didn't answer, he explained by hand, running his fingers down her neck, her collarbone, skimming the love bite on her right breast.

She covered his hand with hers. "It felt good at the time."

He smiled devilishly. "Did it now?"

Her heart opened when he teased her like that. They could be any couple, cajoling, teasing, playing with each other—and tempting fate. Their lives were tied up with Helene and Reggie's. And Aurora's. They had no right. . . . "Reilly."

"I never noticed how often you bite your lip."

She'd never noticed how good soap tasted until he ran his finger across her lower lip. She clamped them shut.

"I love you."

"You didn't seem to this afternoon," she whispered. "After we—"

He looked at the water.

She wanted him to look at her. "Is it always going to be this uncomfortable?"

"As long as I can't say what I'm feeling."

"I don't love you." She didn't want to. That part wasn't a lie.

"I'll take my chances."

She smiled sadly, tracing a damp hand over his scar. "You've taken too many of those."

His hands closed on her arms, lifting her to her feet. "I could never have enough of this. Let me love you, lass."

She shook her head, wet tendrils of hair slapping against her shoulders. "I can't promise you anything. I don't know how long I'll be here."

She'd always be here, Reilly knew, her spirit haunting this house as surely as it would haunt him if he didn't convince her to stay. He lifted her out of the tub, her body slick and fine. He gave her nowhere to go except into his arms. His soaked clothes stuck to him everywhere they touched.

She untucked one of the buttons on his shirt. "I can't give you what you want."

He lifted her chin with his thumb. "It's what I want to give you. Let me do this the way we should have today."

She gave a delicate snort, her expression sassy this time. "I wasn't exactly complaining."

"I stopped too soon."

"You were angry."

"I don't like pretending."

He held her closer, thigh to thigh, her long narrow toes curling on the tips of his perfectly polished shoes. "I wanted to love you, but I couldn't without telling you. You don't have to promise me anything, or put me up against your loyalty to the little girl. Just let me love you."

He kissed her long and slow, feeling her quiver in his arms. A day ago he couldn't have imagined holding her this way, loving her. And yet the road seemed longer than ever, their wires in more danger of being crossed. There were so many factors beyond their control. He put them out of his mind. Tonight he'd love her the way he should have from the start.

He kicked the towel toward the fireplace. The thick animal rug wouldn't be long enough for both their bodies.

Melissa touched it gingerly with her toes.

"Don't like tiger skin?"

"Aren't they an endangered species?"

"Thanks to people like the sixth Lord Darby, I'm afraid. He brought this one home from India in the last century."

"As long as it isn't the third lord's wife," she muttered.

They laughed together, the tension shimmering into nothingness like bubbles in a bath. He introduced her to the feel of fur beneath bare skin.

She felt the afternoon marked on her body, not just

in love bites but in familiar tingles. New sensations re-
doubled the old. No other man had ever made her feel
so safe and so threatened at once. Bodily safe, emotionally bare. He was stripping her of all her defenses, and
she was letting them go.

He strafed her with uncounted kisses, intimate
touches. When he rose, she longed to pull him back to
her, her arms and legs entwined with his. Reluctantly,
she let him go. Standing over her, he stripped off his
clothes then turned out the lights.

The room grew warmer, more womblike. Firelight
flickered red and hot. Candlelight glowed a cool blue off
the glazed tiles. Reilly reached into the cabinet in the
corner, finding more candles, more matches, a small foil
packet he palmed for the moment.

Melissa lazily turned her head as he lit each candle,
their wicks hissing and jumping to attention, growing in
stature as their flames grew. She watched his body,
sturdy and thick, the shadows delineating the well-
formed muscles, his animal grace.

"If I didn't know better, I'd say you were seducing
me again."

He looked at her womanly smile and caught the faint
traces of doubt in her eyes. She'd raised her knees, her
fingertips circling the skin of her abdomen. Her temporary shyness couldn't hide the flush between her breasts,
the dare that glittered in that smile. He was in love with
a very complicated woman. Loving her would be simple
by comparison.

He saw to the details first, letting her gaze rake him
as he moved about the room. He placed a final candle in
the diamond-paned window.

"She didn't die here, did she?" Melissa asked. "The third lord's wife? He didn't chain her up or anything."

Reilly eased himself down beside her. "She met her lover here. For nearly twenty years they met. They could never marry."

"Is that such a tragedy? They had each other."

"Only on the sly."

Propped on one elbow, he curled his free hand over her straying one. He twined his fingers with hers the way he had on the helicopter's throttle. He wanted her to feel in control now as well. Bringing her hand to him, he kissed each finger, laving her palm with his tongue. Then he showed her how to touch him, when to move, and when to hold still.

Her intuition was wicked. He gritted his teeth as she nearly drove him over the edge.

"I warned thee," he said. "I intend to love you for as long as it takes." He'd love her until she couldn't deny that the feelings between them were real, until she knew she was his.

Her hand slowed, her smile wide. She released him to run her hands up his chest. Raking her nails down his back, she urged him toward her. "Then we'd better get started."

NINE

Melissa stood on the steps of Bedford House. Miller had telephoned from the Rolls; they'd be arriving in ten minutes. Inside, the house was a flurry of activity. Cook had luncheon prepared. Crowley had the paths raked and edged. The maids had fresh sheets on all the beds and flowers in every vase.

Reilly had delivered her flowers personally, a bouquet of roses, two red and three white. The white symbolized the days he'd come to her. The red symbolized the nights. If Miller hadn't called ahead, they'd have still been in her room, Reilly's hand grazing her hip, trespassing between her thighs—

Standing on the steps of Bedford House nervously touching the buttons on her blouse, she marveled at their changed relationship. The intervening days hadn't dimmed their lovemaking before the fire in that tiny exotic bathroom. Fierce and proud, he'd stolen her breath with his urgency. Then he'd stolen her heart with his sudden tenderness, parting her by degrees, an almost imperceptible cleaving. Her sensitive body had registered every inch, his shaft filling her until her body rebelled at how thick he was, how deep he meant to penetrate. He settled into long slow strokes that built to a raging unquenchable fire.

She'd turned her face away. She couldn't bear it. It was too much like love was supposed to be. His utter control only emphasized how undone she became so near the edge. Tears raced down her cheeks as she begged him to move faster, to take her. At last he'd branded her his in a shuddering climax that rocketed through them both.

He'd never done it since.

They met in hallways, doorways, a cobblestone archway near the stable. Every time was like the time in the cottage. For her and her alone. While he cherished and ravished her, he kept his distance and his promise: He wouldn't sleep with her until he could call her his. Except for that one taste, that one thrilling example, he'd withheld that part of himself until she was nearly desperate with wanting him.

In the weak English sunshine, she sensed him take his place beside her at the foot of the stairs. He coughed discreetly. She heeded the warning.

Out of the corner of her eye she noted his faultless aplomb. His coat was no longer askew, his tie no longer drooping and untied as it had been moments before upstairs. His body, as she knew intimately, was firm and rigid. She still felt its hot impress against her belly.

Reilly coughed into a gloved fist.

She realized she'd splayed one hand across her midsection. She dropped it to her side. She could take lessons in decorum from him. She thought of all the other lessons he'd taught her in just three days. "How long before they get here?" she asked mildly, noting the other servants collecting around them.

"Five minutes."

They were the soul of propriety. For three days she'd seen to Helene's correspondence in the daytime, joined the servants at supper, and acted above reproach. Then she found Reilly in a deserted part of the house or he found her on a hillside. Time was short. Discovery imminent. She trusted his knowledge of how the estate ran. He trusted her to maintain her composure whenever they were in public.

It should have been easy. It was torture. She loved him and couldn't tell him. It would be better for both of them if, when it ended, they could both walk away unscathed.

But he said he loved her. He'd proved it in a hundred ways. Couldn't she love him back?

"Don't dream," she commanded herself, refusing to misinterpret those long looks when he'd finished with her body, trailing his hands over it, studying her as if he'd memorize her forever.

On the front steps, he caught her longing gaze and gave his head a subtle shake.

Her shoulders tensed. How could they ever maintain this charade? How would she fool Aurora? The child saw through every kind of adult phoniness. She'd know Melissa had changed. Would she feel threatened? Left out? Deserted? Melissa dreaded giving the child the impression she mattered less, that she was loved less because Sally had found someone she loved more. "I mean me," she said sharply.

"Pardon me, Miss?" Reilly inclined his head toward her.

She avoided his concerned gaze. "Nothing."

The imposing Rolls rounded the final curve of the park. As it glided to a halt everyone on the steps stood a little taller, waiting for Miller to hop out and open the doors.

Melissa straightened, feeling the stretch of faintly aching muscles. Her breasts were tender and sweetly heavy. Her legs shook. Desire heated her from within like coals glowing on a grate. While the day held its breath, she combed back a wisp of hair, touching her lace collar to make sure Reilly's latest love bite was hidden. She unconsciously reached for his hand.

He avoided her error by neatly stepping forward. "Welcome home, Your Lordship. I trust your trip went well."

Reggie beamed as he emerged from the automobile. Miller handed Helene out of the back seat. Reggie immediately folded her arm in his. "Wonderful time, Reilly. Wonderful. Crowley, Melissa. Greetings all."

"Hello, Melissa. We missed you terribly," Helene crooned.

Aurora popped out of the car, rushing pell-mell past her mother. The little blond tornado hit Melissa full stride, hugging her close.

Suddenly all of Melissa's worries vanished. How could she think of anything but this bundle of energy and brightness, this giggling whirling comet blazing into her life? "Did you enjoy your trip, puppet?"

"We saw *The Secret Garden*! And Trafalgar Square. And the British Museum. It has all these stones from ancient tombs and dinosaurs and Tuten—Tutie—Tutu—"

"Tutankhamen?"

"Yes! Do you know him?"

"Only by sight."

"He was all dressed in gold and had this mask that must've weighed a thousand kilos—"

Melissa smiled at Helene. "Welcome back."

Helene heaved a melodramatic sigh. "She's been saving all this up for you, I'm afraid. You'll be positively inundated with anecdotes."

"The child was perfection," Reggie stated. "A pleasure."

"And such energy!" Helene added. "I never realized the wonderful way you keep her occupied."

Melissa took her cue. "We'll go to the nursery, if you don't mind. You can tell me all about it there, puppet."

"Do remember to join us for dinner," Helene called over her shoulder as she and Reggie departed.

"Yes, ma'am, we shall." Melissa grinned at her chattering charge. "You sound as if you have all of London squeezed into your head."

"Oooh," Aurora moaned, clamping her hands to her temples. "All of London in here?"

Melissa rapped on her forehead then tapped on her lips. "It went in there and it's coming out here."

Aurora buttoned her lip for all of five seconds. Then she spied Reilly helping Miller unload luggage from the Rolls and snagged his sleeve. "You should have been there, Reilly. A bomb went off in the City. It knocked over a double-decker bus!"

"We heard about it on the radio, lass. Luckily no one was hurt."

"Papa said we couldn't go see it. I wanted to."

Melissa and Reilly shared a look. "You should call him sir," Melissa gently reminded her.

"He said I could call him Papa. Or Reggie. But Mummy said Reggie wasn't proper for family."

"Family, eh?" Reilly unloaded another suitcase.

"You must have gotten along pretty well," Melissa said.

Aurora tugged Reilly and Melissa toward her, bursting to relay an urgent piece of information. They bent so close, their heads nearly touched. "Mummy really likes him," she whispered.

"Does she?" Melissa murmured. This close she could smell Reilly's aftershave, the starch in his collar. She noticed the speckles of gold in his amber eyes.

"What do you think?" Aurora demanded.

Reilly stood, tugging on his vest. "I think a wedding might be exactly what this place needs."

"Don't go getting her hopes up," Melissa scolded.

"I thought that's what hopes were for," Aurora replied. "It wouldn't make much sense if hopes got you down. Would it, Reilly?"

Melissa was in no mood to be charmed by a precocious five-year-old. She shot Reilly a warning glance. "Go ahead, contradict me."

He considered her combative stance and decided discretion truly was the better part of valor. "I said *a* wedding was what this place needed. Did I say it had to be *theirs*?" He fixed her with a look that could light candles.

Melissa's heart nearly stopped.

Aurora wanted to know who was getting married if not Mummy.

"Nobody," Melissa snapped. She grabbed Aurora by the hand and stalked toward the house.

Reilly's hearty laugh followed them all the way to the

nursery. A wedding indeed! She wasn't laughing. She would *not* get her hopes up.

Aurora's sensible attitude echoed in her heart. *But isn't that what hopes are for?*

"Is the lass asleep?"

"For the duration."

The clock in the main hall chimed eleven. Reilly stood beside Melissa in the nursery door as she cast a last look at the sleeping child. His hand rested on her lower back, familiar, strong, suggestive, taking it for granted she'd come to him when her work was done.

She hadn't intended to, not with a full house. But the moment Aurora's eyelashes kissed her cheeks good night, he'd materialized from the shadows. Melissa knew she couldn't resist him. She could love him every way possible, but if she let him know, he'd never let her go. Reilly wasn't that kind of man; he took care of what was his.

In the nursery doorway, he caressed her cheek with the cool backs of his fingers; it didn't ease the fever glowing there. A glancing touch, a touching glance, was all he needed to arouse her, sending her blood pulsing through her veins.

She stared at the sleeping child. "This isn't as safe as it was before."

"I know."

She turned on her heel and stepped into the hall.

He followed, speaking softly. "The countess is sharing His Lordship's chamber tonight."

Melissa wasn't surprised. She'd seen them at dinner. Their infatuation was all the more reason to give Aurora extra attention. Melissa had read to the child for an extra half hour, partly to settle her down, partly to delay the inevitable meeting with Reilly.

She stopped outside her own door. Denying him entrance was futile. He had the key. "What do you want?"

He let his body say it. He closed in, pressing her back against the wall. His lips teased hers, grazing lightly, skipping from brow to lashes to cheekbone. "You're warm."

"The wine at dinner."

He pressed a little harder, looking her in the eye.

She couldn't tear her gaze away any more than she could stop a strangled whisper from escaping. "You do this, you kiss me and tease me. Why won't you love me?"

"I could ask the same of thee."

"You refuse to make love to me."

"I have been."

"You know what I mean."

"Can I sleep with thee?"

"As long as you're gone when Aurora wakes up."

"Can I sleep with thee for the rest of time?"

"You know that isn't possible. Helene—"

"—and Reggie. They're in love."

"That could end tomorrow."

"Or it could last forever. What does that have to do with us?"

"Everything. If Helene leaves, I'd have to go."

"I want you here. And here."

He wasn't listening. He dragged a drugging kiss down the side of her neck. Untying the sash of her terry-cloth robe, he reached inside. He cherished her body through the nightgown Aurora had brought her from

London. It was flannel and modest as a schoolmarm's. He treated it like a negligee of sheerest silk. "I love you."

Knowing what was coming made it all the harder to resist. He touched her and she melted, her body quivering in anticipation. "Then love me."

He groaned and opened her bedroom door, ushering them both inside. Their legs tangled, her slippered feet in danger of being trod on. Reilly lifted the hem of her nightgown until it brushed her knees, a handful of fabric crushed in his fist. "I'll love you the best way I know how."

"Don't stop."

"I'll never stop. Do you believe me?"

She couldn't deny what his hands did to her, how her whole body came alive for him, ready and heated and moist. He touched her with his thumb; electricity jolted through her.

"Do you believe I love you?" He touched her again. Again.

"Yes. Please." Her knees nearly buckled, her nails biting into his biceps as she held on.

He went down on one knee, kissing her until she shuddered and arched back. "Tell me you love me."

She couldn't, no more than she could stop this rush of desire coursing through her, driving her faster and farther. Intense, consuming, she gave herself over to it. His words blurred. The room spun. The last shuddering impulses subsided and she crumpled in his arms.

He reached up to wipe the damp hair from her temple, whispering her name until she recovered. She tangled her hand in his hair, yanking his head back with sudden ferocity. Without a word she bent and kissed him, her mouth open, her tongue brazenly tangoing with his. Taking the fistful of nightgown into her own hand, she pressed against him. "Love me," she breathed.

She felt his effort at control, the rigid posture, the barely contained power. She was tempting the devil himself, unleashing something she might not be able to control. "I want you."

"Are you mine?" He took her face in his hands when she insisted on tantalizing him with her lips. "Kisses aren't answers. Tell me."

He was near the breaking point. She could take him there, *make* him love her. "Stay the night."

"I will. On one condition."

"True love is unconditional."

He uttered a short curse. "Love is commitment or it's nothing at all."

She curved her hand on the taut cords of his throat, feeling him quake. "Is this nothing?"

"It's got to be more than sex between us. I love you."

She was beginning to hate the sound of those words, the obligation they implied. A cold shiver ran through her. She staggered backward. "If you won't make love to me, go."

Thoughtfully pleating the folds of her nightgown between his thumb and finger, he put her back together, tucking her in.

She slapped his hand away, marching to her canopied bed.

"Sleep well," he said.

"Go to hell."

He chuckled as he opened the door. "A complicated woman all right."

She whipped a feather pillow at his head. He caught

it with one hand. Neatly plumping it, he set it on an antique chair. "Good evening, Miss."

The second one landed on the closed door with a thud. "And stay out!"

The rest of the week Melissa spent in the nursery, teaching Aurora to re-create Tutankhamen in watercolors and working in brief history lessons about Egypt. She succeeded at everything except forgetting Reilly.

It was humiliating, having a man profess to love her and never go beyond caresses—even of the most intimate kind.

Why couldn't she be happy with what they had? They were good to each other. He was gentle, passionate, generous. He always put her needs first. That's what drove her to distraction. Despite the wickedly thorough things he did to her, he continued to hold back, giving her everything while taking nothing for himself. He called it love. She called it foreplay. Nights and days of it. No wonder she felt restless and ragged and totally on edge.

" 'for play," Aurora announced.

Dear Lord, she hadn't been thinking out loud, had she? "What did you say, dear?"

"We had steak dinner. B'fore the play. It was wonderful; the play. Do you know any of the songs? It was sold out, but Reilly got us tickets. Reggie says Reilly can do anything."

Melissa gave her a sickly smile. Reilly can and did do everything—except make love to her.

Aurora studied her nanny, solemnly placing the back

of her small hand against Melissa's forehead. "You look wan, my darling. Have you been sleeping well?"

She laughed weakly at Aurora's perfect imitation of her mother. She was growing up so fast. "I have been up a few nights." And down. And inside out. When she wasn't with Reilly she tied herself in knots trying to decide what to do about him.

"Have you been painting?" Aurora asked, changing subjects faster than summer lightning.

She'd painted herself into a corner. She loved him. She just didn't believe it could last. And damn her foolish heart, she was beginning not to mind. As long as they had days and nights together, as long as she could amass memories like the ones she held close to her heart— She only hoped it was enough to get her through the rough times to come.

She asked Aurora to bring her her portfolio, showing off the drawings she'd done for her. The picture of the cottage charmed the little girl as Melissa knew it would.

"You like it too," Aurora declared. "I can tell by the way you look at it."

"It means a lot to me, puppet."

"Would you like to live there?"

If only she could. But a home and man who truly loved her were too much to ask.

Maybe it was ending already. For the last three nights Reilly hadn't come to her room. She didn't fool herself into thinking he'd actually obey her demand to stay away. He'd suggested they meet at the cottage, asking her to steal away for an hour any afternoon and meet him there. She hadn't. She glanced at the clock. He was probably waiting for her now.

Was this what it would feel like when life separated

her from Reilly for good? Her dry eyes took in every detail of the nursery. The emptiness nearly suffocated her.

Miserable, determined, she set down the portfolio and ordered her paint-stained charge to get cleaned up for tea.

None of the love she'd seen had ever lasted beyond infatuation and the debris of disappointment. Love never lasted; children did. The only time he'd made love to her, Reilly had made sure he was well protected on that account. If she went to him in the cottage, would he love her again as he had that once? Or would he torment her, torturing her with what they might do if only she promised to love him, in sickness and in health, for better or for worse—

Her mind insisted that he'd never actually asked her to marry him. Her heart knew he'd never settle for less.

A tiny hand waved in front of her staring eyes. The spell broken, she ruffled Aurora's hair. "What's the matter?"

"We've got a visitor."

"A what?" She turned.

Reilly stood in the open door, impeccable as always. Melissa wondered if anyone else saw the invisible weight that rested on his shoulders lately, the tension etching lines around his eyes.

Her heart swelled. "Did you want something?"

His anguished look said it all. He needed every ounce of reserve to maintain the facade. "I wanted to know where to place these." He wheeled in a tea cart overflowing with flowers.

Her breath caught in her throat. "Which bunch is for us?"

"They all are." He handed her the card.

She scanned it, blushing furiously. She flattened it against her chest before the little one could see it.

"What does it say?" the child asked.

Her hand shook as she tapped Aurora's nose with the envelope. "Don't be nosy."

Hands clasped firmly behind his back, Reilly rocked on his heels and stared into the middle distance, a good soldier facing a better firing squad. "The flowers are from me, lass. I've decided to take the liberty of wooing Miss."

"What's a woo?" Aurora asked.

"It's what I—" He coughed into his fist. "Excuse me. It's what His Lordship has been doing to your mother. Sending her flowers, inviting her on picnics, pouring her wine."

"Holding her hand?"

He glanced at Melissa. "If she'll let me."

"Smooching when no one's looking?"

Melissa released a huff of indignation. "It's clear someone's been spying again."

Aurora blithely evaded the charge. She stepped up to Reilly. She looked like a miniature version of himself, hands clasped behind her back, posture perfect as she paced back and forth before him, a little general reviewing her troop. "Do you intend to send more flowers to Miss?"

"Yes, I do, lass."

"What about balloons?"

"If she'll have them."

"And candy? She likes candy, you know."

His thousand-yard stare darted slightly to the right. "Indeed?"

"Not nuts, though. She likes the soft-center ones." Reilly bent forward to confer when Aurora lowered her voice to a confidential tone. "She bites into them. Little bitty bites so no one will notice. That's how she knows which ones are soft."

Reilly snapped to attention once more. "Candy it is, lass."

"And one more thing. You've got to call her something else."

"Is Miss insufficient?"

"She'll answer to just about anything. But Mummy calls Reggie something special. He's her inam— imam—" She frowned.

"*Inamorata*," Melissa repeated through clenched teeth. "It's Italian."

"*Inamorata*," Reilly repeated, tasting every syllable.

"What is that?" Aurora asked, looking from one adult to the other.

It was Italian for lover. Reilly thought quick before announcing gravely, "It means snookums."

Aurora grinned. She glanced back and forth, coming to the obvious conclusion that her grim-faced nanny and her tin-soldier butler needed a little more advice. "Reggie bought Mummy chryssy—chry—chrys-san-the-mums! In London. A whole room full."

Reilly knew. He'd ordered them. That's where he'd gotten the idea for today. If he could woo a countess, he ought to be able to woo a nanny.

Unfortunately, the nanny wasn't playing along.

"No flowers," she declared. "No balloons, no picnics—"

"I thought the child might like a picnic."

"Oh yes!" Aurora clapped her hands.

Melissa bundled the girl to her side. "And no using the child! You are not pulling these tricks on me, Reilly. We agreed."

"And which agreement would that be?"

The one that said their affair wouldn't interfere with their jobs. The one that said he wouldn't lower his voice the way he had just then, wouldn't send her smoldering looks the way he was right now. The one that said he'd never reach for her hand and caress it suggestively with his thumb.

"I'm in the middle of a lesson." She tilted her head repeatedly, indicating their sharp-eyed little witness.

"Do ye have a crick in your neck?" His hand went directly to the source, kneading her neck in a way that sent shivers down her spine. "Your mistress seems warm to me, lass."

"I *told* her she looked pale!"

"Aye. She does." His gaze bored into Melissa's. "We can't keep something like this a secret from the lass, can we, love?"

"Then we can't go on," she replied, suddenly breathless. "I mean, we can't talk about this, not in the middle of the nursery."

They couldn't look at each other this way, think these thoughts, feel these feelings. "We shouldn't," she added.

Reilly thought a moment. He plucked a rose from the pile on the cart then got down on one knee to present it to the child. "A princess sees much and says little. We trust to your discretion, Your Highness."

"Thank you."

"You'll not give away our secret?"

"Never." Aurora tapped him on the shoulder with the rose. "You may rise."

Reilly did so, a smile curving his lip. When he faced Melissa his expression grew hard and stubborn, his gaze determined and thoroughly bloody-minded. He wasn't backing down an inch.

He raised her hand to his lips. "I promised to love thee. Before I do, I mean to woo thee."

"Am I being warned again?"

"You're being won."

TEN

"So this is your idea of wooing. I take it it's meant to replace—other things?"

Reilly looked at her long legs encased in the skin-hugging fabric of a pair of off-white riding breeches. She sat her horse like a pro, her small rear end bouncing lightly as they cantered down a bridle path on the eastern edge of the estate.

Aurora trotted a few paces behind, the little girl chattering instructions to her pony as they went along.

Reilly stared fixedly at the stones in the path. Fresh air and exercise would never appease the desire heating his blood. Unless he wanted those desires plainly apparent inside his own breeches, he'd better keep his mind on other things.

He urged his horse abreast of Melissa's. "I thought it best if we kept our distance for a while. Considering our chaperon."

"She doesn't miss much."

"I missed you."

She gripped her horse's sides with her thighs, unintentionally spurring it on. When she reined it in, the mare tossed her head. Reilly got the feeling Melissa would have loved to do the same.

"You're the one who's stayed away lately," she said.

"You threw me out."

"You refused to make love to me."

"I thought that's what I'd been doin'."

"Do you think all I want is to have you kiss me? Touch me everywhere? Caress me as if I'm some porcelain statue?" Her cheeks flamed at the very memory. "I'm a woman. If you mean to love me—"

"You're a woman all right."

Her eyes flashed. "And what does that mean?"

He edged his horse closer to hers, their legs almost touching. He fixed her with a searing look. "It means your body is warm and soft and I can fill my hands with it. When I hold you to me, your pulse races. I smell the sweet scent of you on my hands. You're no statue. If you were, I could take you to my bed and never fear. It's the woman in you I don't know."

She reined her horse to a halt. His did likewise. "Are you saying you don't trust me?"

"You're blocking the path!" Aurora's pony trotted around them, clopping up ahead. From beneath her black riding helmet, her blond ponytail switched like the pony's. She whoa-ed the animal to a halt. "Why are we stopping?"

"That was my question," Melissa quipped, daring Reilly to answer.

"I thought we were going too fast," he said.

Aurora looked completely stumped. "It's no fun if you can't go fast."

"Sometimes one has to go slow," Reilly replied, his

eyes never leaving Melissa's. "You have to learn how your animal behaves."

"That's not so hard," Aurora said. "You say giddy-up to go forward and whoa to stop."

Melissa lifted her chin at a saucy angle. "Makes sense to me. I've been saying giddy-up for days."

Reilly chose to explain himself to Aurora. "Let me put it this way, lass. I've ridden this particular horse just once. I've a feeling we could go far together. But before I take her over any jumps, I need to know her personality a little better."

"Do we get to jump?" Aurora asked eagerly.

"Not you, lass. That's for older riders."

"I'll say," Melissa muttered.

Aurora shrugged and headed her pony back down the path. Reilly cautiously slanted a glance Melissa's way. Their horses loped a quarter mile down the path. "Are ye not speaking to me now?" he asked.

Melissa scanned the trees along their route. " 'Never ridden this horse'?" she repeated dryly. "Think you could come up with a more insulting metaphor?"

"I didn't mean—"

She raised one gloved hand, stopping him in mid-apology. Princess Anne couldn't have given him a colder shoulder. Melissa hid the twinkle in her eye. She had every right to get huffy about his animal comparison. For some reason his patient explanation to Aurora, combined with his tense hold on his horse's reins, had roused her sympathy. He was trying, treading as fine a line as she was.

For the moment she held on to her advantage. "I don't care to talk about it," she said.

He scooted forward in his saddle. "Talking's what we

have to do. We took the physical part too fast, it got away from us."

"Like a runaway horse? We need to pull back the reins, is that it?"

"Aye," he grumbled. "It was a piss-poor choice of words and I regret it already."

Reducing Reilly to bad language was such an unexpected turn of events, Melissa nearly choked. Rattling him gave her a giddy sense of power.

"I want to know more about you," he rasped out. "That's all I meant. If you're going to be takin' offense at the least little thing—"

"You implied you didn't trust me."

"You told me not to."

And she'd meant it. Playtime was over. Her voice softened. "You shouldn't get attached to me, Reilly. My job is looking after Aurora. If she leaves, I leave." She gave him a grin. "That's common horse sense."

He muttered another curse. Giving up on words, he gripped her wrist. The sudden move made her horse skitter to the side. He held on. "I want to know more about the woman I love than what makes her back arch and her breath catch in her pretty throat. Is that sayin' it right?"

Melissa frantically scanned the path for Aurora. The child was yards ahead.

For once in his life, Reilly didn't seem to care who saw or heard. "I want to know all of you, Melissa. The sexual part was just gettin' in the way."

"You want to tame me before you ride me again."

He released her with another black curse. He slapped her horse on the rump, making it leap forward. She urged it on even faster, closing the distance between her and Aurora, dashing through the strips of shadow and light cut by the sun's rays.

By the time Reilly met up with them again, Melissa was whistling. She wondered if the English knew this song.

Aurora did; she happily supplied the words. "The old gray mare, she ain't what she used to be, ain't what she used to be—"

Judging from Reilly's scowl, the English knew it.

A half hour later, crossing rolling fields and hedged-in forests, Reilly dismounted to walk Aurora's pony around a stone fence. Melissa took the same path.

"Jump the fence," Aurora called as Reilly remounted his horse.

"I don't think that's the horse he wants to jump," Melissa commented dryly.

Reilly's scowl deepened. Melissa's grin transformed into a musical laugh. A strange elation buoyed her spirits; she was actually having fun. Teasing him, simply spending time with him, made her feel happy and free, careless and reckless. Maybe sex had gotten in the way. His explanation helped ease the unbearable tension building in her these last few days. But if he thought she'd agree to overlook her attraction to him, he wasn't the rigorously intelligent man she knew.

He was more, she thought, uneasiness warring with cautious exhilaration. He hadn't come to her lately because he wanted to love her more not less. He loved her. And he meant to woo her.

A corner of her heart told her to beware. She still

couldn't guarantee them a future together, not when her duties lay elsewhere.

"Whoa," she murmured. Her horse paused. Reilly wanted to know more about her. He thought it would deepen the relationship. Melissa knew it might end it. She practiced various ways of explaining her mixed-up life to him. They all ended the same way. *So you see, Reilly, I'd be a very bad risk.*

She was so involved in wording her explanation, she barely registered the gleaming Rolls-Royce gliding down the country road in the distance. A few minutes later they rounded a bend, trailing deeper into the forest. Her head snapped up at Aurora's cry.

Beside a babbling brook a table sat covered in lace and linen. In the faint breeze, two candles guttered. Silver shone in the flickering sunlight.

"A picnic," Aurora shouted. When Reilly helped her dismount, she threw her arms around his neck in a hug.

Would Melissa ever get used to his ability to create magic? She watched him for a long moment as he approached. "You're a very special man, Reilly."

"Just doing my job. Miss."

She forced the corners of her smile downward. "Is wooing me such a hard job?"

He dragged in a long breath and let it out slow. "Let's just say it's no day in the park."

She laughed out loud at his honesty. Swinging her leg over the saddle, she hopped to the ground. She slapped her unused whip into his hand. "You wanted a horse to ride. She's all yours."

The mare snorted and nuzzled her nose against Reilly's shoulder. Melissa laughed wickedly and sashayed toward the table.

Reilly grumbled something unintelligible, watching her lean flanks lovingly encased in those off-white breeches, her long legs embraced by trim black boots. Minding his manners had never been so difficult. If the child hadn't been there, he'd have repaid her nanny's sass with a roll on the riverbank. His kiss would take the starch out of that stiff neck. He'd turn her to putty in his hands. Explosive putty.

He tied the horses' reins to a low branch. Playing the perfect butler, he pulled out Aurora's chair, then seated Melissa to his right. "Wine?" A bottle of chilled white sat in an ice bucket.

Aurora leaned across the table to whisper to Melissa. "More woo."

"I got that part." She winked.

Aurora extended her glass to be filled.

Reilly smoothly substituted sparkling water. He uncovered the dishes one by one. "A French sauce for the chicken. Cook is experimenting with Continental cuisine in honor of our guests."

"Mummy says the English would be wonderful cooks if they didn't boil the flavor out of everything."

Melissa wagged a finger at her. "What she means, Reilly, is that Helene appreciates a more cosmopolitan menu."

"No offense taken, Miss. I believe we can accommodate the countess. With practice, everyone's needs can be met."

"More metaphors?" Melissa asked.

"Looks like broccoli to me," Aurora said.

Reilly spooned out a serving of vegetables, directing his words to Melissa. "What I mean, Miss, is that people can change. They can adapt."

"Add spice to new dishes."

"Or let them cool if they're too hot."

"Don't want anything boiling over."

"Some things need to be savored on the tongue. Given time."

"Aged?"

"Ripened."

She sipped her wine. "One likes to know the ingredients that go into a dish one intends to consume. Is that what you've been saying?"

"If you like."

She more than liked. She looked into his eyes and saw love and patience and humor. She saw a man she wouldn't hurt for all the world. For that reason, she had to be honest. He didn't know her very well—she hadn't let him. But if she did, he might give up on her altogether.

She clutched her napkin in her lap, daintily popping a tiny carrot in her mouth. It melted like butter. "Some recipes are passed down through generations. Like long-held family secrets."

"I'd be honored if you shared your recipe with me."

"I never knew you liked cooking," Aurora said.

"Hush. The grown-ups are talking now."

"Okay." Aurora picked at her broccoli.

Melissa spared Reilly a short glance. "Love, for instance. There's a spice I avoid."

"Mind if I ask why?"

"Perhaps because my mother overused it in everything she cooked."

He studied her for a long moment. They could speak in code only so long. To understand more he'd have to wait for a time when the child wasn't present. He reached for Melissa's hand, the one clutched in her lap. He brought it to the table, then to his lips. Despite Aurora's keen interest, Reilly held on.

"The wine's making your cheeks pink," Aurora observed.

"Aye." Reilly touched Melissa's cheek, letting her feel the contrast between his body temperature and hers.

Her eyes fluttered shut. "I thought you weren't going to do this," she whispered.

"This is a different kind of loving."

It was all the same to Melissa, a longing that tugged at her heart, an unquenchable need every bit as powerful emotionally as physically. Her fear that it wouldn't last was changing bit by bit, to a fear that it would never be.

"May I be excused now?" Aurora scooted her chair back. "I'm going to brush my pony."

Reilly dropped Melissa's hand to pull the chair out. "All right, lass. But no riding him till we're done."

"Yes, Reilly."

He sat back down.

Melissa thoughtfully watched Aurora chatting to her pony as she brushed its neck. "We shouldn't be so familiar when she's around."

"It does a child good to see real love. Gives her something to look forward to when she grows up."

"Maybe I never looked forward to it because I never saw it."

"Was your parents' marriage that bad?"

"I was so young, I don't even remember it."

"Your mother's remarriage, then?"

She laughed without smiling. "Which one?"

He waited, patient as stone.

Melissa dabbed at her lips and took a deep breath.

Might as well get it over with. "My mother married five times. As of last count. Aren't you going to laugh?"

"It's unusual."

"It's ridiculous. She'd chase after every 'prospect' she found, looking for romance, passion, something, anything better than what she had. After a year or two of marriage, things lost their rosy glow. They always do. She'd pick fights, sulk, accuse her husbands of playing around. She'd start looking again, looking for someone who saw the same stars she did, heard the same violins. Love never lasted. I began to think it didn't exist at all."

"Until?"

"You don't miss a thing, do you?"

"I try not to."

"I thought love was a fantasy women created, a fantasy doomed to fall short."

"Until you met me?"

"But who's to say it will last?"

"I promise thee—"

She sat back. "Don't. That's what wedding vows are for. I know; I was a bridesmaid four times. Correction; flower girl for Sally's second, bridesmaid for weddings three, four, and five."

"Where was your father?"

She heard the censure in his voice. Reilly would hold fathers equally responsible for their children's care. That's the kind of man he was.

She smiled wistfully. "A lot of adults complain their fathers weren't around enough when they were growing up. In our case, *I* wasn't around enough. He's a good man, but he has another life; that's all. A second wife. A daughter named Dianne. The only times I saw them were when Sally dated someone who didn't like children.

Then I'd be farmed out. And honeymoons, of course. She'd go on a honeymoon, I'd go to Iowa. Except when she married her fifth husband."

"What happened then?"

"I was sent away permanently. To boarding school. One of the finest in Europe; I can't complain. Nothing but the best for Dr. Waverly's new wife."

The best school wasn't a home. Reilly set his knife beside his plate. The meal had lost its savor. "I take it you haven't seen her in a while."

"Every now and then we're in the same city at the same time. I don't hold grudges, if that's what you mean. Sally isn't like other people; I know that. I can even see her point of view. Honeymoons are no place for children. I'd have been in the way."

Reilly cursed under his breath. "Children aren't in the way, they're part of it. What would life be without them?"

"You don't have any."

"I plan to."

Melissa believed him. Reilly meant what he said. He listened, too, weighing her every word the way he listened to her sighs whenever he touched her. She was absurdly grateful, even if she did think of it as just another example of his attention to detail. He didn't run away, didn't exhale one of those long-drawn-out sighs a man sighed when he'd come close to making a major mistake in his life.

Reilly was tactful, concerned. When she most needed it, he allowed her to change the subject with a short laugh and an indulgent smile. "See yourself as a family man, Reilly?"

"I saw you sitting in my kitchen. I knew you belonged there, with me. As for children, a blind man could see you love them."

"I love this one."

"She isn't yours, is she?"

Melissa canted him a startled smile. "Certainly not. There are ties every bit as strong as biology, you know."

"The past, for instance?"

"How so?"

"You're her. You see yourself in her, a little girl who needs to know she'll be loved, that the people she loves won't leave her."

"Ah, psychoanalysis. Do your talents never end?"

His love wouldn't. "Have I hit a nerve?"

"You're getting close. My mother's affairs may have affected my sense of security as a child, but everything has its bright side."

"Such as?"

"I learned to rely on myself. I'm very strong when I need to be. I'm a rock where Aurora's concerned. She'll never have that kind of insecurity. I managed, Reilly. I managed just fine."

Excepting for the fact that she couldn't recognize love when she saw it, he thought, she'd managed exceptionally well.

"Helene is a good mother," she added, despite the fact no one had asked. "Aurora adores her. When she's settled she's very attentive. Her choice in husbands has been her weak point. Prince Albrecht and Monsieur Trenchement were more interested in their playboy lifestyles."

"His Lordship is genuinely fond of the child."

"You think so?"

He couldn't resist the vulnerability that snuck into

her voice, the hope and fierce protectiveness that came alive whenever Aurora's happiness was at stake.

"She'd be happy here," Reilly said. "Reggie's serious about his responsibilities. And his commitments."

"Kind of like you."

"A man stands by his word or he isn't a man."

She stared at her goblet, running her finger along the gold ring encircling it. "I'd say you've stuck by your rules pretty firmly these last few days."

"You know I want you."

With every nerve in her body. "I believe you. I believe *in* you. It's the happily-ever-afters I don't trust."

"Do you trust me?"

Yes.

He leaned in close. Each tasted the other's breath as their words crossed.

"Don't give up on us, Melissa. That's the only thing that frightens me."

"I can't imagine anything scaring you."

"There's a lot we have to learn about each other."

She loved him and he loved her. Wasn't that all they needed? She suddenly had the overwhelming desire to blurt out the truth, to rush into his arms and give him anything he wanted.

The wind stirred a strand of hair onto her cheek. He gently smoothed it back. With that one gesture she believed in all of it. For one day, one afternoon, a man loved her exactly the way she was. If forevers were possible, she'd love this man forever.

They laughed and teased, their horses cantering toward the stables. Reilly and Melissa challenged Aurora to a race they shamelessly threw, letting her pony trot across the finish line first. Aurora said it wasn't fair— they were too busy smooching to pay attention.

With utmost dignity, Reilly agreed completely. Melissa had told him of her past with such a stricken look on her face, he'd expected a direct connection to Lizzie Borden by way of Jack the Ripper. In a way, her life had been worse. He suppressed a surge of anger every time he thought of her flighty mother. However, Melissa wasn't her mother. What she'd given him in the last two hours was more important than any number of revelations.

She'd given him clues to herself, wires leading to connections. As a child, she'd seen adults betray each other in the name of love until she associated love with losing people. If he could prove to her love lasted, she might believe in a future for them.

As they clip-clopped into the stable yard Reilly caught sight of Reggie and Helene standing outside the stalls. They'd be Exhibit No. 1. Heads together, hands entwined, they'd been working out every aspect of a potential marriage. Reggie had told him that much.

Reilly swung down from his horse, helping Aurora from hers. A groom appeared, leading the pony to its stall. Aurora followed.

Melissa sat her horse until Reilly came around. He reached for her waist; she slid into his arms. Their bodies barely touched. The moment her boots touched ground his hands fell to his sides. Only their eyes conveyed the happiness of the afternoon, the intimacy of secrets shared.

"See?" he said, nodding toward their respective employers framed in the archway at the far end of the stable. "Things do work out."

"We still have to mind our manners."

"Discretion is my middle name."

"I never did find out your first."

He never got the chance to tell her.

The sharp echo of a woman's raised voice sounded the length of the stable. "I don't see why you *assume* I'd feel that way," Helene snapped.

"But darling—" The rest of Reggie's mild reply was lost in the nervous shuffle of horses in their stalls. Melissa and Reilly froze, neither saying a word.

"Don't you take that tone with me," Helene retorted.

"That is not a tone," Reggie said, his words clearer as his voice rose. "That is a response. If you didn't fly off the handle all the time, it would not be necessary for me to chastise you like this."

"Oh Lord," Melissa murmured.

Reilly's jaw clenched. He knew it was a poor choice of words. Man-to-man, he sympathized entirely. Even from this distance he recognized the controlled desperation of a man losing everything he'd dared dream for in life. Logic was not the god of love. Clinging to it, Reggie succeeded in driving the woman he loved farther and farther away.

"Perhaps chastise is not the correct choice," he intoned, hastily wrapping himself in that mantle of stuffy correctness he'd shed since Helene's arrival. "Rather, what I meant to say—"

"Say nothing!"

Melissa flinched as Helene's riding whip cut the air. Her heavily accented voice pierced it. "I will not marry a man who seeks to rule me. I've had two such men in my life, one a prince who thought a title would hold me, the other who sought to buy me with his billions, trillions. What do I care? I wish to be loved, not owned. I will not be taken for granted!"

"But darling, you fly off the handle—"

"Ha! I'll show you flying. Reilly! Where is that pilot? We will fly to Heathrow *tout de suite*. Aurora! Melissa!" Helene stormed out of the stable and toward the house, Reggie in nervous pursuit.

The dust settled. Melissa and Reilly stood mute. The horses stomped in their stalls. A groom whistled low, shaking his head as he unsaddled the last horse.

"Where's Aurora?" Melissa asked softly. "I've got to find Aurora."

Reilly gripped her wrist. She swung around, her eyes flashing. "If she heard—"

Reilly nodded toward the end of the stable.

Two stalls down from the site of Helene and Reggie's battle, Aurora stepped out from behind her pony, a brush in one hand, her riding helmet in the other. Deathly silent, she looked to her nanny.

Melissa ran to her, wrapping her in her arms. "It'll be okay, puppet."

"But I liked it here," Aurora whispered, her cheek damp against Melissa's.

"So did I, honey. So did I."

Reilly's stomach coiled, his fist clenched. "They can work this out, lass. Adults argue."

"Mummy never apologizes."

"What matters is that they love each other," he insisted. "If they do, they'll solve this."

"And if they don't?"

He stared bleakly into Melissa's upturned face. "If they don't, it doesn't mean we can't."

Melissa stood, Aurora's tiny hand in hers. "If Helene leaves, I'll have to go."

"They don't own you."

She gave him a tender smile, shaking her head from side to side as the tears glimmered in her eyes. "Unfortunately, neither do you. I'm sorry, Reilly."

She led the little girl outside, speaking to her in a low voice as they hurried toward the house.

He'd done it again, falling in love with a woman who couldn't be his, and all because he'd agreed to woo someone he didn't even know.

He took the back way into the house, needing a moment to think. He disagreed with Melissa—their lives were not out of their hands. Life was too short to give up without a fight. The only question was, whom did he fight?

ELEVEN

With controlled violence, Reilly swung the bedroom curtains open. It was four P.M., teatime all over the former British empire. High time he had a talk with His Lordship.

"Over here," Reggie muttered, hidden in the depths of a wing-back chair. He swirled a snifter of brandy in one hand, a half-empty bottle in the other. "Is she gone?"

"The countess was in the library the last I saw, sir." She'd been arguing with a tight-lipped Melissa. Reilly hadn't had time to eavesdrop, he had other arrangements to make. "I called the local airfield. The helicopter won't be ready until morning. Scheduled maintenance has the engine in pieces at the moment."

"Maintenance? You never allow anyone to touch that machine except yourself."

"Always a first time, sir."

There was a long pause. "You wouldn't be stretching the truth, would you, Reilly?"

"Always a first time," he muttered to himself. He

took the dangling bottle from Reggie's hand and set it on the side table with a bang. In Reilly's estimation the emotional blow had staggered His Lordship more than any brandy. "You can't give up, sir."

"Don't see I have much choice, old chap."

"Apologize." Reilly's drill-sergeant bark elicited mild surprise on Reggie's pale moon of a face.

"Apologize? Dammit, man, I've done nothing wrong."

"You will, sir, if you let the countess go. I've never seen His Lordship so—so bloody happy, if you'll excuse the term. I'd hate to see it all go to waste."

Reggie considered Reilly's brusque appraisal of the situation. "Realize you've put a lot of work into this. Appreciate the pep talk. But the lady's up and dumped me. Bad luck. Bad show. Not much I can do."

Nor could Reilly, or so it seemed. He'd never felt so out of his element. How the hell would he know what had Helene so fired up? He'd been wooing the wrong woman all along. He marched across the Oriental carpet at half-parade pace, muttering her name until he hit upon a solution. "I've got it, sir. Buy her something, a token—"

He lurched from his chair. "I am not going to *buy* the woman, Reilly. Helene has feelings. She may seem all froth on the surface, but I assure you she has very deep, very complicated, womanly-type feelings. And I'll be damned if I know what they are. Thought I was taking her riding, and the next thing I know I'm accused of taking her for granted!"

Reilly grumbled in his throat.

"Is that bad?"

"The worst, sir. There's no defense. If you agree,

you incriminate yourself. If you disagree, you prove her point."

"But I told her it wasn't true. I pointed out all the things I've—you've—bought her. The things we've done for her."

"And?"

"She accused me of thinking she only cared for money. By the time we reached the stable, she was about to draw and quarter me with her riding whip."

"I noticed the whip, sir."

"Pardon me?"

"A momentary slip, sir."

"I bought her that bracelet, Aurora's pony—"

"Do you like the child?"

"Absolute angel. Reminds me of her mother."

"And you love the countess?"

Reggie strode to the window, the look on his face all the confirmation Reilly needed. "That's not something a gentleman discusses, as a rule."

"Quite right, sir."

Standing at the window, Reggie lifted his snifter to his lips then paused in midmotion. Outside, Melissa trailed a wildly gesticulating Helene through the garden. Were those streaks of tears on Helene's face? Did her eyes look puffy?

Standing shoulder to shoulder with His Lordship, Reilly couldn't tell. Hoping that Melissa was imploring her mistress to give it one more try, he silently cheered her on.

"You think buying her a bauble would do it?" Reggie said at last.

"They aren't baubles to a woman, sir."

"Yes. Suppose it's the thought that counts. Dash it

all, does she think I think of anything else? The woman's on my mind night and day." After more rumination, Reggie spoke the question worrying both men. "And if baubles fail?"

"Then do something else," Reilly replied heatedly. "And something after that. Never give it up, sir, not if you love her."

Reggie looked at his butler in a whole new light. "You've gotten quite involved in this affair."

"In a manner of speaking, sir."

Reggie drew his mouth into a severe line. He strode toward the telephone, slapping a directory into Reilly's hands. "Get me that jewelers in London, the one down the street from the Ritz."

Reilly sprang into action. "May I tell them what you're interested in? Another bracelet? Something larger?"

Reggie squinted into the distance, thinking hard. "Something smaller."

"Smaller?" Reilly's mouth went dry. If Reggie did too little, Helene would be twice as insulted. They'd never win her back.

Reggie elaborated. "Something ring-sized, I should think."

Reilly flipped through the directory. He'd learned long ago to identify the faintest tremors in his hands. He ignored this one as he jabbed a finger at J for Jeweler: Wedding Bands, Engagement Sets. "Very good, sir. Very good."

It was a terrible idea. As if chasing after Helene and trying to talk her out of leaving hadn't been failure enough, Melissa's next bright idea involved bringing Aurora down to dinner in order to convince the child everything was fine.

The dining room had never been more cavernous. Reggie didn't show and Helene begged off with a sick headache. Two maids brought their apologies from opposite ends of the house. Even Reilly failed to appear, delegating another servant to attend the meal. Dejected, Melissa took Aurora by the hand and led her to the kitchen, where they ate in strained silence with the staff.

Silverware clinked against plates as Melissa brooded. Genuinely hurt, Helene claimed Reggie had slighted her. Melissa wanted to grab her by the shoulders and shake her. If slights were the only sins Reggie ever committed, the woman had nothing to cry about. Taken for granted? Losing a man you loved for no reason except that you were afraid to tell him was a hundred times worse.

She'd finally opened her heart to Reilly, unburdening herself of her embarrassing past. He'd met her revelation with stoic acceptance, his steady patience quietly, relentlessly urging her on to ever greater risks. She'd been about to take the biggest risk of all and tell him she loved him when this happened.

Ironic. She'd always been the first to run, refusing to get involved with anyone "just in case." Now that disaster had struck, she found herself staunchly defending these topsy-turvy feelings, gathering them to her breast like precious jewels. She would not let some run-of-the-mill tiff between Helene and Reggie ruin what she and Reilly had. She wanted his love even if it scared her, even if her own carefully protected heart, her carefully constructed world was turned upside down in the process.

More than anything, she wanted to talk to him.

A rumble of thunder rattled the windowpanes. Rain lashed at the glass. Branches scraped stone walls. The light clicking of a key in a lock penetrated the storm's howl. Reilly shoved the door open, the wind whipping his yellow mackintosh.

Melissa leaped to her feet and ran into his arms. He stiffened subtly, aware of their audience. Behind her, conversation stumbled to a halt. No doubt looks were traded among the staff. Not a word was said.

She didn't care. She'd broken one of his cardinal rules and she didn't care a whit. She saw the storm in his eyes. Her own heart was filled to bursting with things she had to say.

He set her back on her feet, his gaze shuttered, inexcusably remote. "Excuse me, Miss."

Stunned, speechless, she stepped away from him. Not for long. A surge of love made her close right back in. It was his love that had given her the courage to claim these feelings. "Where have you been?"

"Running an errand, Miss. His Lordship asked me to fly down to London."

"At this time of night? In this weather?"

Haverford muttered from the table. "Thought the chopper was out of commission."

"Word travels fast around here," Reilly murmured in reply.

"Apparently not that fast." The crew-cut security man glanced toward Melissa.

Cook smiled at her gravy as if it were an old confidant. The under-housemaids gave each other knowing winks. Crowley buttered another biscuit, minding his own business.

Reilly remained indifferent to Melissa's hovering. He removed his coat, absently shrugging her hand off his arm as he did so. He didn't see her flinch; he'd made sure of that, averting his face as he stepped across the kitchen. He hung the mac on a peg, donning his butler's black coat. "I overestimated the extent of the chopper's repairs. We pieced her together and got her off the ground all right."

"Did you fly over Robin Hood's house?" Aurora asked.

Reilly petted her hair. "Sorry, lass, no time."

Left standing in the doorway, Melissa folded her arms across her middle. "You should take every chance you get." Her voice surprised everyone, including her.

Reilly's gaze didn't meet hers. "You might be right, Miss."

"Never give up, that's my motto."

"Mine too. On occasion. Is the countess still bent on leaving?"

"I haven't spoken with her lately." *I wanted to talk to you first.*

Cook rose, spooning Reilly's dinner onto a plate.

"Don't bother, Mary," he said softly. "I've some business with His Lordship first."

"Don't let it get cold, love."

"I won't."

And yet he was willing to let Melissa stand there and slowly turn to stone. She didn't know whether to fume or burst into tears. She couldn't understand why he was acting this way.

A very real possibility ran its icy fingers down her spine. Perhaps his flight to London and back had given him time to think over what she'd said. Maybe he'd decided it was safer not to pursue a relationship with a woman who didn't know the meaning of love.

She knew it now. Her heart practically shouted it. But how could she say it? She should have known he'd dislike any blatant shows of affection in front of the staff. Maybe that simple transgression explained his distance.

Reilly paused by the mirror near the servants' staircase, tugging his vest into place, straightening his tie. He patted a small package in his pocket.

Melissa closed the distance between them. "She loves him, you know."

His neck stiff, his back stiffer, he barely turned his head. "The countess and His Lordship?"

Her gaze scoured his face, the weary lines around his eyes, the determined creases near his mouth. "I know she does, Reilly. Very much."

His amber eyes met hers. "And he loves her. I'm sure of it."

Then why was he acting this way?

He shook his head slightly, deciphering her imploring gaze and silencing any question she might voice. This was not the place.

"We've got to do something," she insisted, stopping him before he could go. "They each need to know how the other feels."

"Then she can tell him."

"Now?"

He glanced over her shoulder at the table of silent diners. "If you'll excuse me, Miss, I have a package for His Lordship."

Her cheeks colored. Her gaze fell. He hadn't understood a word she'd said. "Of course. If you want to leave, don't let me stop you."

For a long moment he stood there, jaw clenched, hand turning over a square velvet box. Sliding it into his pocket, he methodically saw to his appearance, shooting each cuff, matching the length of white on the left to the white on the right. Then he marched upstairs.

Melissa sat at her end of the table. She hadn't really expected him to drop every facet of professional behavior the moment she declared her love. The man was preoccupied, as concerned with Reggie's crisis as she'd been with Helene's. He'd just flown to London and back, for Pete's sake! The excuses piled up until she reached the one she feared most; he'd changed his mind about loving her.

Standing tall, she announced it was past Aurora's bedtime.

"But you've barely eaten," Cook replied. "Let me give you a plate to take with you."

"No, thank you. Good night every one." She ignored the burst of conversation that erupted the moment they left the kitchen.

At the foot of the main staircase, Aurora tugged her hand. The library door opened. Reilly emerged. He looked as if he'd expected to find her there, as if he'd been waiting, steeling himself against seeing her again. His back soldier straight, he bowed and requested their presence.

Melissa squeezed Aurora's hand. She refused to be intimidated by his self-possession. If their love never came to anything, she could handle it. She'd left people all her life. But she wouldn't deny how she felt, not any longer. "I have to talk to you."

"Perhaps later would be more convenient."

"Now."

"Melissa!" From a corner of the library, Helene swam into view, a blissful smile on her face. Two air kisses brushed Melissa's cheeks. "You see, my darling, everything worked out. I told you it would."

Helene told *her?* Melissa blinked rapidly. It didn't help that the hand waving happily in front of her face sported a ruby the size of a thumbnail.

"Reggie's asked me to marry him!"

"And you said . . . ?"

"Yes!"

Melissa's breath rushed out of her. Tears sprang into her eyes. "That's wonderful, ma'am."

Aurora wriggled between them, embracing her mother's waist. "Mummy's getting married again!" She tore herself away to hug Reggie.

He patted her on the head so enthusiastically, Vandyke barked and tried to get in on the action. "There now," Reggie rumbled, "things have a way of working out, just like Reilly said. Knew it would. Knew it would."

Melissa turned to Reilly, the tears in her eyes adding to the sparkle of her smile. "Did you do this?"

He scowled almost imperceptibly, casting a warning glance Helene's way.

"He brought me my ring," Helene exclaimed. "He flew to London just to pick it up. Isn't it marvelous? And *so* thoughtful." She caressed Reggie's cheek. "Thank you, my dear."

Aurora danced over to Reilly. He bowed nearly double, letting her throw her arms around his neck. "Welcome to the family, lass."

"Thank you, Reilly."

Melissa stepped to his side. "Thank you, Reilly. For everything."

"Just doing my job, Miss."

"Is that all it was?" She tried to sound playful. Fear gnawed at her heart, making the words she'd wanted to say seem foolish and naive. Reilly had won the woman Reggie wanted. His "job" was over.

She tugged on Aurora's hand. "Time for bed, puppet."

"You won't share some champagne with us, Melissa?"

She declined Lord Darby's invitation. "Sorry, sir, not tonight. The little one will be up until dawn as it is."

"I'm going to have a new papa."

"I know, puppet, but it's bedtime now. Don't worry, he'll still be here in the morning."

And so would Reilly. And every day after that. If he pulled away from her, how would they work together, how would they live in the same large house? She had to think.

"Of course you'll help us with the wedding," Helene called after her. "We've so much to arrange."

"I'll call your attorney first thing in the morning, ma'am."

"That dreadful dull man. We must have caterers lined up, too, florists, planners. You remember my marriage to Monsieur Trenchement? I want just the opposite."

"Yes, ma'am. I know all there is about arranging weddings."

Reggie signaled his butler. "Reilly. Get my lawyer on the horn first thing in the A.M. A prenuptial agreement, that sort of thing, provisions for Aurora, college funds, trusts. Want to see the child taken care of."

"Yes, sir."

"You and Melissa will handle things splendidly, I'm sure."

Reilly wasn't so sure. He watched Melissa collect Aurora and head for the stairs while he poured the happy couple two glasses of champagne. He retreated into the background while they made their plans and cooed their apologies.

Apologizing to Melissa for his brusque behavior meant he'd have to explain it to himself first. He'd come within hours of losing her for good. Flying back from London, he'd wondered whether she'd even be there, whether Helene might have simply ordered Miller to drive them elsewhere. He'd pictured an empty nursery, a silent bedroom. Seeing Melissa the moment he'd walked into the kitchen had moved him beyond words.

So why had he treated her so unfeelingly, like the heartless bastard Clare had once accused him of being? Because Melissa had been right all along; they had no future. As long as an argument between Reggie and Helene could undo everything they had, love wasn't enough. Maybe he couldn't afford a ruby, but a ring was the only answer.

Melissa practiced her calligraphy in the library at a large antique table. Normally a wedding of this size would take months to arrange. Helene had decided to break the rules and marry impulsively, precipitously, depriving the world press of a chance to gape and gawk outside an English cathedral.

She'd asked Melissa to hurry the invitations by designing and hand-lettering them herself. At first Melissa combined the task with handwriting lessons for Aurora.

The child quickly grew bored in the stuffy atmosphere of the library and chose riding lessons instead. Melissa couldn't complain. After two weeks hunched over a table she'd barely reached the Gs in Helene's enormous address book. The wedding was only two weeks away.

"You're like a monk in here copying Bibles."

She bit her lip as Reilly entered. She hadn't seen him since the announcement, except in passing. He saw to the lawyers who arrived daily in their stocky black cars, trekking through the house, droning in the library, closeting themselves for hours at a time with Lord Darby. With his knowledge of the estate, Reilly had proven himself indispensable yet again.

She missed him like mad.

"Busy?" she asked. She kept it light. She'd been trying to let him know through jokes, teasing remarks, and fleeting smiles in crowded hallways that she was sorry for the way she'd thrown herself at him in the kitchen. She'd never do it again. Honest. But dammit all, when was he going to give her the chance to tell him?

He set a red leather-bound book on the edge of her table. "His Lordship's address book. I've taken the liberty of marking in pencil who shall receive invitations and who shall receive announcements."

"Efficient as always. You must have stayed up nights getting this done."

Her heart froze as he reached for her, seemingly against his will. He traced the circles under her eyes with a fairy-light touch. "I'm not the only one losing sleep."

She shut her eyes tight, her lashes skimming his thumb. "What happened, Reilly?"

He plucked at the creases in his slacks, sitting as far

from her as the Edwardian sofa allowed. "I needed time to think."

"What did you decide?"

His eyes roamed the book-lined walls. "We'll need to order some garlands for the shelves. The guests will expect every room to be decorated in some festive fashion."

"And flowers? I've missed the flowers."

He fastened his gaze on the intricate Oriental carpet.

"You said you loved me, Reilly. I have a right to ask if you still do."

"You were right about our lives not being our own. With things the way they are, we've no future."

"That doesn't mean I won't fight for what we have."

"And that would be?"

She set her pen down, scooting over beside him. His shuttered look fell to the place their thighs touched. No one was better at hiding his feelings than her Reilly.

Leaning her elbow on the back of the sofa, she trailed her fingers through his sandy-colored hair, watching the gold threads glisten. She tried with all her heart not to acknowledge the tension hardening his features. She gathered her courage before it scattered to the four winds. "When Helene and Reggie fought, I realized I had to love you more not less. If this could fall apart at any moment, we need to seize all our time together."

"Is loving enough?"

"Loving is everything." He'd taught her that. It had started here, with a cheek she'd reached out and touched. She pressed her lips to it, sensing the nerve that jumped there. She balanced her forehead against his taut skin, inhaling the unique scent of him, musky masculine aromas melding with the tang of something distantly familiar, an ancient smell she associated with special occasions. "You've been polishing silver."

Anything to settle his nerves while he worked up his courage. "I want more than love from you, Melissa."

She gave him a sweetly pleased smile. "Then meet me at the cottage."

"I can't."

"I know you're busy. Do you think I've been doodling in here?"

"It's being dismantled. The interior, at any rate."

Shocked, she drew in a shallow breath. "The cottage? That was our place."

"We're moving the security monitors to a room over the stables. It's a better location for a security post, more centralized. The cottage will be empty."

She sat back, her long legs tucked under her protectively. "Why do I have a feeling you're moving *me* out of your life too?"

He wanted to move her into it. First, he had to find the words. He'd come to propose. Asking her to marry him should have been the most joyous day of his life. Instead he found himself groping, searching for simple words, clutching at details, garlands, invitations, the trivia he'd filled his days with for the last two weeks while he wrestled with how to ask her, what to offer her.

Asking a woman to give you her life was like choosing which wire to cut in a booby-trapped mine. If she said no, that would be it, it'd be over.

He rose from the sofa and walked stiffly to the double doors. He directed a few words to a maid who'd lingered too long in the hallway, swatting a bronze Adonis with her feather duster. Having secured them some privacy, he shut the doors behind him and crossed back to the sofa.

He unconsciously patted his vest pocket as he sat. He should've thought of getting her a ring when he'd flown to London—there hadn't been time since. It was completely unlike him to overlook an important detail like that. It made him feel jittery and off balance. Like a man in love. He'd felt that way in Northern Ireland once. This time he wanted guarantees before he pledged his heart and soul.

She'd turned her back to him, her fingers straying through the pile of invitations. "There's no need for all these preliminaries, Reilly."

His heart shriveled. She was turning him down before he'd even asked.

"I understand." She laughed, a crooked grin on her face, a look in her eyes she didn't want him to see. "Your master's getting married. Your job is done. Romancing me was a bonus. It was also a wonderful example of your foresight. You do think of everything. When Helene thought of going, I was there to talk her out of it. Because you'd made me fall in love with you. Well done, Reilly."

He gripped her shoulders, turning her to him with undisguised force. "You were never my job."

She stared him down, refusing to be rebuked for fantasies that sounded paranoid even to her. "How am I supposed to know? What am I supposed to think? You won't talk to me. For two weeks you've avoided me."

"I've been thinking."

"Am I a part of that?"

"You're all of it."

"Then why won't you let me in? Why did you shut me out like this?"

"I wasn't sure what you'd say."

Her searching gaze scanned his troubled one. "I'd say what I've been trying to say for two weeks. I love you. Is that so scary?"

"It is if you can leave me anytime."

TWELVE

She took a long, deep breath, collecting herself.

He reached for her, unwilling to let her withdraw by even an inch. He buried his fingers in the silky warmth of her hair, his lips inches from hers, his breath hot on her face. "I need to know you'll stay, no matter what happens with them. I can't have us hanging by a thread, Melissa."

"I love you."

"Tell me you're mine."

"I am."

"Forever?"

She laughed, indulgently this time, running her hands over his face. "You know I don't believe in forevers. But I believe in love. You made me believe it. You're a wonderful man, Reilly."

"Are you happy here?"

"More than I've ever been."

"Then stay. Marry me."

"You know we can't."

He cupped her face in his hands, more precious than any silver. "I'm not joking. I want you here."

"You have me. Just don't ask—"

"Why not?"

She stepped out of his embrace. Somehow he'd known all along it would fall apart fast, with one wrong move, one word. "I can't."

She retreated down the canyon formed by the sofa on one side, the long table on the other. Her fingers strayed over the piles of invitations.

He had to close the distance, had to try. "Why not?" he demanded.

"Because marriages are forever," she said simply. "And forever doesn't last."

"It can."

"If you believe that, then you'll believe in Helene and Reggie's marriage. As long as that lasts, I'll be here. I'm not going anywhere, Reilly."

"Unless the child goes."

"I'm here. We're here. Don't let it get away. Why can't loving me be enough?"

The words sliced like shrapnel beneath his skin, cutting no matter which way he turned. He'd get down on one knee, he'd do anything. But he couldn't get past her resistance. "I promised myself I'd never sleep with a woman I couldn't call mine."

"We already made love. Once."

"It was only a taste. We could have a lifetime of loving. I'd never leave thee."

"What about Aurora? I promised her I'd always be there if she needed me. I can't go back on it because I've fallen in love."

"And if I need you?"

Her eyes shimmered. "She came first."

He took a deep breath. "What you're saying is, I'd have to learn to accept that."

She blinked rapidly, stemming her tears. "If you loved me, you'd accept me the way I am. Please—"

He backed away, posture perfect, hands limp at his sides. He couldn't. He couldn't pledge his life to someone who didn't belong to him, who didn't want to. "Then we might as well stop here."

She bowed her head, touching the objects on the table, the folded vellum invitations, the neck of the ink bottle. She pricked the knifepoint nub of the pen with her finger.

She'd made a terrible mistake. But with him standing there waiting for her reply, she couldn't decide what was worse—refusing to marry him or falling in love with him in the first place.

"Is that it, then?" he asked.

A pang penetrated her confusion. She had the terrible feeling she'd never hear his accent again, the blunt Yorkshire inflection he used only for her, the mask he dropped for her. The next time they spoke, and all the times after, she knew he'd use his proper voice, the conventional accent he used to address visitors, guests, strangers.

Her throat constricted. She picked up the red leather book he'd brought with him, flipping through the gold-edged pages. "You wouldn't happen to know how to address the twice-divorced wife of a former ambassador who's now married to a duke, would you?"

He didn't speak.

"Come on, Reilly. You know everything."

"Except how to make this right."

The pages blurred with her unshed tears. He stepped toward her. She waved him away. "Maybe you should go. Please. Will you do that for me?"

He'd do anything. He curved his hands into fists, forcing his face into the aloof mask he assumed when duty called.

Melissa sank onto the sofa, hunching over her work. She slid a blank sheet of paper before her. A tear spattered it.

Reilly pretended not to see. Discretion, he called it. His eyes traced the lean elegance of her spine, the defeated slope of her shoulders. He saw no way to change her mind. "I can't love you *temporarily*. It's forever or it isn't love."

"Oh, I think it's forever." She sighed wistfully. "But I love you too much to make promises I can't keep. I'm sorry, Reilly."

A clock ticked on the mantel. Motes of dust fell through the slanted sunlight like falling stars, their light extinguished when they hit the shadows. It was a big house. It'd be a lifetime's work keeping it up. He'd thought that the first day he saw it. Bedford House would be enough to keep a man busy, to stop him thinking too much, wanting things that didn't belong to him, things he had no right asking for.

"I'll leave you to your work. Miss."

He strode to the door. Every step of the way he waited for her to speak. The carpet muffled his footsteps until his heels clicked on the hallway's marble floor. Behind him her pen scratched over the heavy vellum paper, tinkling now and then against the ink bottle.

He closed the double doors behind him, standing with his back against them. Like a man before a firing squad, he pictured every rifle trained on his heart. A muffled sob sounded on the other side of the door. His fists tightened on the brass knobs.

They were too much alike. Each had made a home by working hard. Her home was with the child; his was here. Unless one of them sacrificed everything they'd worked for, they were destined to remain separate, like the blade-thin parallel lines Melissa drew on her pale paper or the squares of marble beneath his feet, perfectly matched, fixed, and unmovable.

"May I help you?"

Melissa spun around. She didn't want him to think she'd been spying in his room. She'd barely trespassed into the servants' wing since their conversation in the library ten days earlier.

He looked terrible. His back was stiff, his face taut, any show of emotion strictly forbidden.

"This isn't what it looks like."

He took the framed photograph from her hands. Before he set it back on the dresser, he ran one finger along the surface to clear away invisible dust. "I saw the little one running down the hall. I expect you were playing hide-and-seek."

"The little scamp talked me into it. She said I'd been working too hard."

"So you have." Reilly didn't have to look at her to see it. He knew her face as well as his own; he'd memorized it in long hungry gazes and fervent stolen moments.

Why had she come? He paced off the length of his bed, absently straightening an already clean room, tugging a comforter Cook had made him, tucking the fold beneath the pillow.

"Four days until the wedding," Melissa said brightly.

Her voice hovered in the air, emphasizing the tomb-like stillness of a room he'd once thought of as home. It felt more like a cell every day.

She tried again. "It seems like every time I turn around you're doing something. Always on the edge of my vision. Always moving away."

"There's a lot of work to be done."

And a lot of forgetting. She'd holed herself up in the library like a monk in a cell while he served dinner to an endless procession of guests. Some days he caught sight of her as he strode toward the garage, seeing to the new security apparatus, checking on the guests' automobiles. He conferred with Crowley regarding flowers and taste-tested the bouillabaisse Cook busily perfected. The only time he didn't see her was in the library or the nursery. Or her room.

Today she'd come to his, thanks to an impish little devil with flyaway blond hair.

Reilly gestured at the furniture, feeling as stiff and stuffy as Reggie. He mentally corrected that—as stuffy as Reggie used to be, before he met the woman he loved. "Is there something you wanted, miss?"

"I hear you're going on the honeymoon."

"His Lordship asked me to accompany them. I'll see to the arrangements in Jamaica. The cottage the duke loaned them in Kingstown needs to be prepared and staffed. His Lordship wants everything top-notch for the countess."

"You'll serve them breakfast in bed every morning?"

"Serving breakfast is part of my duty."

The conversation ground to a halt, hung up on the idea of waiting on other people's happiness while theirs slipped away.

Melissa edged toward the door, dawdling, trying to make it look like boredom, trying desperately to think of a reason to stay. How could they make love when they couldn't even make conversation?

The moment her hand touched the doorknob, Reilly spoke up. "Cook's been giving me lessons. She's turned me into a passable chef."

Melissa smiled, relief flushing her cheeks. "I'm not surprised. I'm beginning to believe you can do anything."

Then why was he losing her? She read the words in his eyes as plainly as if he'd said them.

He turned away. "I'll be gone a month."

One step, one small step closer. "I'll miss you."

"You'll be here with the child. That should make you happy."

Her progress stopped. She tried to put things in perspective, to let them both know she could handle this. "Don't worry about me. I've been left behind before when people went on honeymoons. My mother made a career of it. Still. I was hoping."

"Hoping what?"

"That with Reggie and Helene gone we'd have a month together, to talk."

He wasn't about to let her dangle carrots in front of him. "I'll be gone a month."

"So you said."

Another uncomfortable silence buzzed through the room like a drowsy fly.

Melissa didn't know what else to say. She belonged

there every bit as much as Reilly; it was absurdly easy to justify. "We were playing. Aurora scurried in here to hide. I tell her giggles are laughter's crumbs, I follow hers like a trail. I didn't realize it was your room."

"So this is her doing."

"I'm beginning to detect a pattern, aren't you?"

"Yesterday she arranged for us to meet at the stable. Two days before that she sent us to the village to post identical letters."

"She asked me last week, 'Where's the woo?' She thinks it's all a game." A game that had ended with the score undecided. "Reilly—"

"Miss—"

She laughed as they both spoke at once. "You haven't called me that in quite a while. As a name, I mean, instead of a barrier."

"It's easier that way."

"We'll be living together."

"In one sense."

"Working together, then. Living in the same house."

"If you don't want to marry me—"

"I can't."

"Then we'll need to maintain some distance."

She tried, damn him. For ten days she'd been trying.

She puttered around his room, running her hands over the iron rail at the foot of his bed. Voices passed in the hallway outside. She was tempted to fling open the door. For his sake she kept her voice low. "I suppose it would raise a few eyebrows if I was seen coming out of your room."

Unruffled as always, he replied that the staff probably wouldn't be surprised. "They're a perceptive lot."

They'd figured out the reason for his bad temper

long before then, Reilly thought. For ten days he'd been angry with vendors and gruff with tradespeople. The bits of advice Cook mixed in with her recipes fell on deaf ears. He was losing every shred of his uncompromising reputation. He was losing Melissa and he couldn't seem to stop it. The life he'd wanted was blowing apart in all directions, like a bomb going off in slow motion. He couldn't catch the pieces fast enough to hold them together.

She headed for the door.

"Would you like a cup of tea?" he blurted out.

She shook her head, but she stayed. When she looked around the room, his heart beat again.

"It's not at all what I expected. I pictured you very Spartan, very military. You've made it a home within a home."

Had he? He saw the plainness she politely over-looked. What good was a bed to a man who'd lost the ability to sleep without a woman at his side? What good were plaster walls, glaring and white without her paintings to lend them color. His clothes hung like ghosts in the closet. They'd once held the smell of her perfume, illicit embraces captured in their fibers. Now they smelled of bleach and detergent, hard water and a hot iron.

She turned from the closet. With his silent permission, she prowled into the next room, surveying the space he'd turned into a cozy den. It looked like a hotel room to him, leftover end tables from other ends of the house, a worn sofa, a lamp with a torn shade repaired and turned toward the wall. A silent television set. A silent radio.

She ambled back into the bedroom. She nodded to

each of the photos lined up on the dresser, absorbing his terse explanations.

"Square-faced lad of sixteen. Not much to look at."

She smiled at the frame she held in her hands. "Is this rugby?" She indicated his broad-striped uniform shirt.

He looked at the muddy field instead, the council houses looming in the background. Bedford House was worlds away from the working-class neighborhood and industrial grime that defined his childhood. He'd found something precious here, order, timelessness, a world worth preserving. Without the promise of her to share it with him, it had become as barren as the trampled fields of his youth.

She set the picture back, running a fingertip over the next.

"My two brothers, m'self, my father."

She grinned at the four men staring out at her as if meeting each for the first time. They all had the square Reilly jaw and stocky build. Robert had a pugnacious tilt to his chin, Michael twinkling good humor around his eyes. Reilly had both their qualities, plus a sense of restraint that set him apart, a watchfulness that studied Melissa like a chalice, or a gleaming sharp razor. Loving her then losing her could hurt him the rest of his life. Letting her go was cutting him to shreds.

He'd pasted a Polaroid to the dresser mirror. The edges curled slightly. "My parents," he said when her gaze hovered on it.

"They look very happy."

"Forty years."

"You told me."

"Did you listen?" He touched her for the first time

in days. He felt her quiver inside, her whole body like a willow longing to bend.

"I have to keep my promise to Aurora. Please say you understand."

"I think I do. Your promise wasn't just to her, it's to the little girl you used to be, the one who got left behind. I'd never leave her, Melissa. When I take a vow I mean it."

"What about Aurora?"

"Her mother can look after her."

"Mothers aren't always the best judges."

"Hers or yours?"

She sighed. "We all carry emotional baggage. I'd be the first to admit I have mine. But I was all grown up when I made a promise to be there for her. I won't break it."

He dragged a hand across his mouth. His past played a part in this too. He'd always wanted a woman who could make a commitment—in Melissa's case it wasn't to him. "My baggage says it has to be marriage or nothin'."

"Baggage can't talk, Reilly. Even Aurora knows that."

He returned her impish smile with a rueful one of his own. "It does when you've lost as much sleep as I have."

"Has it been that rough?" She caressed his cheek.

He held bombsite still.

"You look tired," she said.

"You look beautiful."

"Tactful as always. I look like hell. My mother would have a fit. Helene's even mentioned it—every day this week."

"Days I should have spent telling you how much I love you." He knew he ought to fight. He'd told Reggie never to give up. But who did he fight? Where did he turn?

Tracing her cheekbone with his index finger, he connected the freckles scattered across her nose like flecks of brown sugar. His fingernail skimmed beneath her fine red lashes, the length and color of an artist's sable brush. Grasping at straws that thin and fine, he asked if she'd been painting lately.

"I stopped by the cottage last week hoping to."

"I haven't had time to clean it up properly."

"I couldn't bear to see it so empty."

He couldn't bear to see her slipping away. Was the cottage all they'd ever have? A handful of afternoons, clandestine meetings in out-of-the-way places? "I'll see to it when I get back."

Their month apart. They couldn't solve anything apart. If only they could hold on.

As if reading his thoughts, she wrapped her arms around his waist, fitting herself to him. "I'll miss you."

He held her fast, not questioning why it seemed natural having her there. Like her first visit to the kitchen, he was convinced she belonged in this room she'd never visited, with him. It was crazy. It was also the surest thing he'd ever known in his life. "Will you wait for me?"

Her cheek to his chest, he thought he felt a shudder. Bracing himself for her tears, he looked down and saw a teasing smile crinkle her eyes.

"I'll wait. Unless Haverford makes me a better offer in the next couple weeks."

"*He'd* keep you safe. And your little girl. He'd probably put tracking devices in her shoes so she couldn't wander off."

"Make hide-and-seek easier."

"Is she the only reason you came?"

Another silence loomed, filled to the brim with things they couldn't say. He held her by the shoulders. "If you go on living here, I want it to be because you want to be with me, not because you're watching over the child. Not because it's your *job*."

He chafed the back of his neck with his partly clenched fist. "Never thought I'd have a five-year-old as a rival. Where is she now anyway?"

"At her riding lesson."

"You feel safe letting her out of your sight?"

"That isn't the kind of security she needs. Besides, everyone on the estate loves her. It's just, if anything goes wrong with her new family, I want her to know someone will be there for her."

"Always?"

"Until she's old enough to manage without me." Melissa held her cupped hands before her, as if holding her love in them, like water dipped from a fountain. "You asked me to wait for you. I will. But that's only for a month. I'm asking you to wait for me too."

"How long?"

"Until she can stand on her own."

His lips compressed in a tight line.

She slanted him a sheepish glance. "One of the first things I noticed about you was your patience. Tell me you'll be there when I'm ready to let her go."

"Is that when you'll be ready to love me?"

Her fingers strayed across his dry lips. Her tongue moistened her own. "I'm ready for that now."

He gripped her arms, drawing her to his chest. She held her breath at his controlled violence. It wasn't the first time she'd seen his carefully constructed facade break and crumble. She was the only one who saw the passion inside the formality. He needed her. He always would.

"If we can't make commitments, we can still make love," she said. "We have that much."

"I don't mean to let you go, lass. Not ever." Denying her had honed his desire to a knife's edge. His body reacted hard and fast. His mouth covered hers, his tongue thrusting inside. When he spoke again his voice was harsh and thick. "You do love me."

"I do." Her breathing grew ragged and faint. "It's been weeks."

He tried not to remember. Holding her in his arms, and holding back, became impossible when he recalled her body rippling beneath his in the tower, her long legs winding around his waist on that fur rug.

His hands ranged over her clothes, his mouth tasting the faintly scented flesh of her neck. All the rules he'd ever made concerning women blew away like dust. One of them had to bend. If he couldn't marry her, he'd love her as if they had. Maybe then she'd see marriage as more than a trap some women sprang on men. It was a commitment freely given—like the body she gave to him.

He kissed her deeply. He opened her blouse and filled his hands with her breasts, running his thumbs over the light brown aureoles' satiny sheen. They pebbled as he took them in his mouth. Details flitted into his mind. "The child won't be back?"

"Not for an hour."

He looked into her softly astonished eyes and his

blood heated. To think he did that to her with no more than a kiss. "And your mistress?"

"Having luncheon with a deputation of local politicians' wives. She won't need me until teatime."

"His Lordship is in the city for the day." He stroked her hair back, feeling the tremors run through her. "We have time."

It might be all they had. He didn't mean to waste a second.

THIRTEEN

Reilly walked over to the door and locked it. He heard her breath catch with the lock's click. The man's face he glimpsed in the mirror was harsh and stony, the mouth grimly set. Stripping off his shirt, he shed the rest of his clothes and ordered her to do the same. She complied, a trace of apprehension in her eyes. A scrap of silk hushed to the floor.

He searched through his dresser drawer for a foil packet. The drawer's swollen wood screeched when he shut it. Melissa winced. Her nerves were as raw as his voice.

"Get on your hands and knees."

A flash of rebellion stiffened her spine. She sat on the bed, tucking her feet under her. "What do you plan to do?" She should have known better than to ask that question in such a husky voice.

"It isn't a plan, it's a promise. Every act of love is a promise."

He intended to cherish her with his body, his hands, his very being. He'd fuel her desire until she ached for him the way he throbbed for her, taking her farther than they'd ever gone. He'd protect her too.

While she watched, he encased his shaft in a thin coat of latex. That finished, he stood beside the bed, thumbing her nipple until it peaked. She covered her breast with her hand.

"There's no such thing as modesty between lovers."

"I know," she said breathlessly.

"We don't have to marry, if that's what you want. That won't stop me wanting everything you are and everything you have. It starts here, Melissa." He reached for her waist, pulling her up on her knees until her body aligned with his. Then he crushed her to him in a devouring kiss, robbing her of all strength, all will.

This wasn't the gentleness she'd come to know. It was passion, domination. An age-old struggle between pride and submission warred within her, toppled by the breath-stealing knowledge of his hands on her flesh. It was the darkness of untold secrets and unexplored desires, sublimation and surrender. Beneath it all, beyond her startled cries and unchecked desires, was the shameless acknowledgment of a woman's power over a man.

She kissed him everywhere he demanded and kissed him some more. When she got on her hands and knees, her hair flowed around her face, a curtain of red streaming with gold. Raising one arm, she flipped it back over her neck, silently directing him to kiss her there.

He obeyed. His mouth grazed her ear, her nape, her spine. His thighs aligned with the backs of hers, his shaft touching her. When he stroked her flanks, she quivered inside like the deep silent ocean disturbed by a rippling wave. His hands ranged familiarly, possessively down the inside of her thighs.

"You're mine," he said. "This is our wedding bed."

Her breath backed up in her lungs. Her throat tightened. The love they'd made before had been coercive, seductive. This was primitive, forceful, all pretense at civilization dropped. "I want to see your face."

Balanced on one locked arm, he bent over her back. She turned to see him until her chin nearly touched her shoulder. It was all he'd give her. Her eyes fluttered closed when he kissed her ear. His free arm curled around her body, his hand stroking her heavy breasts, flattening against her abdomen, pressing up, in, lifting her, readying her.

He thrust forward. Too stunned to utter a sound, she clenched all around him. With his second thrust a moan tore from her, honey flowed. Her body quaked, threatening to give way beneath his raw power. He thrust deeper than she'd ever felt.

The world shuddered and danced, the earth itself undulated. He wrapped both arms around her waist and sat back on his heels, pulling her with him. Her back rested against his chest. She collapsed against him, her breath coming in shuddering spasms.

Impaled, she couldn't escape. His freed hands ranged across her body. His fingers tangled in her coiled hair. He touched her nub and she cried out, writhing and arching against him.

He covered her mouth with his hand. She bit it. He grunted; he welcomed it. He drove her higher and higher, stripping away every layer of self-protectiveness, refinement, and decorum they'd ever hidden behind. They exploded together, eruptions shaking them both, concussive waves of sensation shuddering through their bodies.

When the last spasm ceased, he dropped his hand from her mouth. "I couldn't let anyone hear us."

"I know," she said with a gasp.

Her limp body balanced on his slanted thighs. She threw her head back, resting it on his shoulder. When she shook her head, her hair cascaded down his back. She sobbed softly, partly from relief, partly from roiling emotions, overwhelming but unresolved, buffeting her in waves. When the emotions subsided, she found his hand and lifted it to her lips. She kissed his palm. "I'm sorry I bit you."

He nibbled her ear. "It felt good at the time."

That won him a startled laugh then a thoughtful sigh. "Love is amazing, isn't it? I never thought—"

He waited.

"I guess I never thought," she said at last. "Never dared dream."

His body grew still. He'd never loved her more than he did at that moment. He tried to hold her without crushing her to him. He'd never let her go.

After a few minutes her breathing grew more even. She unclasped his arms from around her waist and led his hands over her body. "I belong to you now." As earthy and unsophisticated as the words sounded, they held the ring of truth.

"Aye. You're mine."

Melissa smiled in quiet amazement, her eyes roaming the white walls, the plain furniture, the man in the mirror holding a woman so close, they could have been one body. She belonged to someone at last. She belonged here. "I love you, Reilly."

He held her for an eternity of quiet. "In four days, I'll be going."

"I'll wait for you."

He kissed her shoulder, licking the salt from her skin.

Fizzy, skittering sensations started low in her body, flowing outward down her thighs. She let them unwind, wondering if he felt them too. They were still joined. "Will you wait for me?"

"For as long as you need me to."

Until Aurora was too old to need a nanny.

Voices sounded in the hall and receded. They separated when the voices died away. Reilly tugged loose a sheet to wrap her in. The tenderness was back, the wild desire abated. He wiped her damp hair from her forehead, a smile curling his lips. "I'll dream of thee."

"Don't ever stop."

"I love you."

"I love you."

They held the matching promise to their hearts. *I'll wait for you.*

Melissa strolled down the gravel path past the circle of hedges and through the shadowed park to the front gate. The postman was late, the box in the stone pillar empty. She decided to wait awhile, listening to the birds chatter in the trees.

The wedding had come off spectacularly. Helene looked resplendent and chic in an off-the-shoulder wedding gown. Lord Darby looked as dignified and aristocratic as any portrait lining the main hall. Aurora skipped down the chapel aisle in red velvet and ribbons, a beaming angel holding a bouquet of baby roses.

Melissa sighed, blushing as she remembered her tears. Reilly had sat in the pew beside her. "I always cry at weddings," she'd said with a sniff.

Ready for any occasion, he'd handed her a pressed linen handkerchief. "From what you've told me, you've had a lot of practice."

"Did you see the way she looked at him?"

"Or him at her?" Reilly looked at her the same way then.

"They really do love each other. I hope it works out."

He'd wrapped her fingers firmly over his arm. "It will, Miss. It will."

The words had been their final good-bye. Between the afternoon they'd made love in his room and the afternoon four days later when Reilly flew Helene and Reggie to Heathrow for the start of their honeymoon, Melissa had had almost no time alone with him. If it wasn't Helene insisting she had to pack more and more clothes, it was Reggie summoning Reilly in an absolute panic over where the devil his riding breeches had got to. They'd been busier than ever. And more in love.

The giddy knowledge that she loved someone heart and soul hadn't blinded Melissa to Aurora's needs. To Melissa weddings meant abandonment, a mother rushing off on another romantic quest. Yet Aurora seemed completely at ease. The child withstood the furor of last-minute details like a trouper, retreating to the nursery whenever the adults got too frantic. Melissa had worried about her for all of ten minutes.

"They'll only be gone a month," she assured her little charge.

"I know," Aurora answered in her grown-up manner. "I told you, when Mummy gets a new husband, I'll get a new father. Until they get back I've got my pony, and the gardens, and you."

Sitting by the estate gate, Melissa chuckled to herself. She wasn't sure she liked the billing order on that list. But Aurora's matter-of-fact attitude eased her mind considerably. She murmured an old promise to herself. "You've got me, little one." And she had Reilly.

Or rather, she wished she had. At the moment Reggie and Helene had him. "Couldn't they just rent a butler in Jamaica?" she asked peevishly. She immediately decided to draw the picture that came into her head: a Rent-a-Butler shop with models on display, black butlers in white coats, white butlers in black tails, Oriental butlers in tan jackets serving orange pekoe tea. Butlers old and new— "And only one Reilly."

He was definitely unique. And if she didn't wipe this smile off her face, every passing lorry would know why. She was a very lucky woman. And for the ten days since the wedding a very lonely one.

She'd gotten a letter from him the day they'd arrived in Jamaica, and another two days later. She had no right expecting another so soon. That didn't stop her haunting the gate.

The postman drove up, saving her further self-pity. He grandly placed the airmail letter from Jamaica on top. Coloring furiously, she thanked him and strode smartly back to the house.

She hadn't gone ten steps before she tore into the blue-and-red-striped envelope. She unfolded four neatly handwritten pages, skipping past the salutation to the opening paragraph:

I assume by now the debris of the celebration has been cleared away. The garlands should be taken down before they dry out. Be particularly careful to remove all leaves and pine needles from the shelves in the library as we don't want them falling out years hence when visitors reach for a volume. . . .

Melissa huffed and riffled the pages. Four sheets of instructions to the staff! Worse yet, what would Cook think when she saw the hasty way Melissa had torn it open? Probably laugh and wink knowingly at a pot of boiling water.

She flipped through the other correspondence. A thin white envelope bore her name, postmarked Jamaica. Her steps slowed.

Dearest Love, he wrote. *My duties are just that. I have a cottage of my own on the edge of the compound. It's empty without you and lonely as only paradise can be. I miss you to my soul. Try as they might, the native girls have been unable to do a thing to ease my pain.*

Ha! She swatted the heel of her palm with the paper. He teased and provoked her for one whole page. Then he described the nights.

Her mouth grew dry. Her heart raced. Her cheeks turned the color of a ripe Jamaican sunset. He'd spoken to her the same way in bed, by turns poetic and earthy, romantic and unashamed. He ended with a pledge, as always, to love her forever.

And so she'd love him, she thought, unable to imagine loving anyone more. Everything she had and was, she'd given him.

Everything except her hand in marriage, her conscience whispered. Everything except forever.

Aurora's voice broke into her thoughts, interrupting the pall that had fallen inexplicably over her day. "Is that a letter from Reilly?"

"What makes you say that, puppet?"

"You're fanning yourself with it."

She glanced down in dismay, the tissue-thin paper wavering beneath her chin. Judging from the heat of the words he'd put into it, the paper probably had scorch marks on it.

"Does he put perfume on his letters? Is that why you do that? Can I smell?"

"No, honey, it has no smell." That was probably the *only* sensual delight he failed to capture on paper. She hastily folded the stationery, almost shoving it in the envelope meant for Cook. She corrected that potential disaster just in time. "Let's go up to the nursery."

"All right."

Aurora had thrown herself into her studies with new enthusiasm. For a while Melissa worried that it was a way of coping with her mother's absence, but, as usual, the child blissfully accepted whatever life handed her.

"Are you ready for your reading lesson?"

"Let's do history. I feel smart today."

"You are smart."

"Would I be smart around other children?"

Melissa hugged her hard. "Even smarter. You've traveled everywhere. You speak French, English, and a touch of Italian. You're gobbling up that math book."

"If I went to school, I'd sit in the front row and take tests and carry a whole pile of books. I'd know everything eventually. All the kings and queens, all the countries, the capitals . . ."

Melissa's mind drifted as the child chattered on. She

lay on a sandy white beach, the sultry tropical air caressing her skin. Palm trees swayed over her, the waves kissing the edges of Jamaica. Reilly touched her bare back, his thumb slipping beneath the strap of her bathing suit—

A small hand tugged hers.

"I'm sorry. What, darling?"

"If I write a letter to Mummy and Papa, will you post it for me today?"

She and the postman were practically on a first-name basis. "Of course I will."

Aurora scooted off to a corner of the nursery to work on her letter. Melissa reread Reilly's letter. He'd totally committed himself to her. Would she ever be capable of returning that love completely? Or would her heart always be divided between loving him and loving this child?

If he loved her, he wouldn't make her choose.

And if she loved him, her heart whispered, she wouldn't have to.

Their month apart should have given her plenty of time to think. Instead, Melissa found herself just living it, relishing the pace of the days, the hum of a well-run home, the busy-ness of Aurora soaking up knowledge like a sponge. Not for the first time she thought of Bedford House as an extension of Reilly, steady, enduring, reliable, home.

They both had prior commitments. With her it was Aurora, with him this house. He couldn't expect her to sacrifice the child to her happiness any more than she'd ask him to leave Bedford House for her sake. And yet, one of them had to bend.

Melissa came to a decision—but then, she came to decisions every day where Reilly was concerned. Her latest involved compromise. If only he'd love her for the time being, waiting patiently until Aurora was a little older. He'd already promised.

That had been in the heat of passion, her doubts murmured.

Reilly never lies, her heart insisted. All the shimmering emotions she'd distrusted so long—hope, optimism, love—infused her with energy. Maybe he would wait, but in the meantime she had to find something to do with herself. Hiking down to the mailbox didn't begin to dissipate the jittery case of nerves that bedeviled her.

She decided to walk to the cottage while Aurora had her riding lesson. The empty shell made her heart turn over. Everything but debris had been removed to the new security post over the stables. Restless, she began straightening, picking up bits of wire and ends of tape, shooing dust off the windowsills.

The next time she visited she came armed with a broom, a dustpan, a bucket, and a mop. Before the week was out she'd commandeered rolls of wallpaper from storage, beautiful old patterns left over from the main house. With Cook's permission she borrowed a few cast off chairs and sofas from the west wing, a couple of lamps. The cottage became such a part of her days, she took Aurora there and let her read aloud while Melissa worked.

The child dubbed it the Schoolhouse. "I'm getting too big for a nursery anyway," she said.

Melissa humored her latest whim. Aurora had an image of school that rivaled Disneyland.

"Cook asked why you didn't bring a bed out here," Aurora asked later in the week.

Melissa twisted on the stepladder, a paint roller in her hand. She glanced at the only room she hadn't redecorated, the tiny bedroom she and Reilly had once shared. "A bed?"

"Cook says no one else uses the place, it might as well be yours."

Hers. The idea bloomed in her like the revitalized cottage. Not hers, theirs. She saw the cottage in a new light. Making the place a home was what she'd been doing all along. Thanks to Aurora, she'd realized it. Thanks to Reilly, she'd found the courage to put down roots.

The thought of losing things didn't haunt her the way it used to. Somehow it had been overtaken by the greater fear of never having them.

She considered the little girl sitting at the desk by the window. Maybe Reilly was right, that little girl was her. But not entirely. Aurora didn't protect herself the way Melissa did. She didn't need to—she had Melissa and always would. Now Melissa had Reilly. Knowing someone loved her was all she'd ever needed.

In five days he'd be back. When he returned she'd do more than promise to stay with him. She'd ask *him* to marry *her*, *for as long as our lives allow*. And the future be damned.

"What are you grinning at?" Aurora asked.

She thought briefly then answered decisively. "I'm in love."

"Well, I knew that."

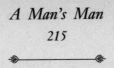

Saturday morning came. Melissa walked up to the main house, her legs shaking, her nerves in a tizzy, only to be informed that Helene and Reggie had decided to spend the day in London before heading back to the estate the following day. Melissa's face fell when Cook gave her the news.

"Of course, our Reilly will be back this afternoon to see to it the house is up to standard for His Lordship's arrival. And your lady's."

"Of course," Melissa said. He'd be back today. She'd known it for a month. She was totally unprepared.

Filled with a sudden desire to flee, she darted a glance around the kitchen. What if he scorned her idea of living in the cottage? What if her marriage proposal fell flat? What if, with his perfect bearing and imposing posture, he simply refused to marry her unless she promised him the kind of forevers he expected?

She was ready to promise him everything she had and everything she was. What she was included her commitment to Aurora. Would he accept it?

Half an hour later she sat in the cottage, her hands shaking as she poured the tea. Footsteps crunched down the trampled path leading from the house. With some heavy-handed hints from Cook, Crowley had gotten the idea of spreading white gravel before the cottage's entrance. "To make it more homelike, love."

Melissa hoped to heaven Reilly saw it that way. It would save her a lot of explaining. All he had to do was look around him. Then he'd take her in his arms. She'd look up at those tender amber eyes and—

A heavy knock landed on the cottage door. Her cup

clattered into the saucer. Wiping her hands on her slacks, she opened the door.

Reilly scowled on the threshold, peering into the dimness. "So you've moved out here."

The words *welcome home* died on her lips.

He brushed past her, careful not to touch her. "I never expected this of you."

She hadn't expected this of him. Struck speechless, she watched him prowl the living room like a caged bear. The heavy oak beams lowered over his head.

He cleared his throat with a grunt. "You can't live with me. Fine. You've decided it won't work. You might be right. But you could have waited until I got home to tell me to my face instead of hidin' out here, takin' to the woods. No matter how scared you are, you've always been brave enough to overcome it, Melissa. Instead I come home to this." He indicated the small room with a sneer.

Melissa's nerves had disappeared, gone somewhere numb. She stood beside the table pouring him tea. "If you'll have a seat, I can explain."

"I told you a long time ago I don't interfere where I don't belong. I belong at the main house. So you made yourself a home out here. That says it plain enough."

"Does it?"

"You've got everything you need. A desk for the little girl. A place of your own." He headed toward the door, eyes fixed on the warped floorboards. A quiet rasp tore out of him before he went. "You could have warned me in your letters."

She blocked his escape, teapot in one hand, cup and saucer rattling in the other. Joan of Arc couldn't have stood straighter or surer. "I didn't think a warning was necessary."

"You're right. You've warned me before."

And loved him a long long time.

She watched the way he pulled his shoulders back, donning his utmost reserve. Reilly might be the perfect butler, but he had his fears like everyone else. He simply managed to hide them better than most.

Not from her. The next time her man got quiet, the next time he used work to exhaust his fears into submission, she'd know why. Despite their mutual promises before he'd left, she'd done the same the last month— working her fingers to the bone fixing this place up, waiting, worrying. He didn't see the care that had gone into it. Not yet he didn't.

"I've made this my home. Would you like to see it?"

He never took his eyes from her face. "I see it."

She nodded past his shoulder. "The kitchen."

Hands clamped behind his back, he swung around. "Aye, it's a kitchen all right."

She nodded past his other shoulder. "The bedroom."

He refused to turn, glaring into her eyes as if he'd lost something and could only find it there. "Melissa."

No. She was going to do this her way. First she had to make a choice. If she set the teapot down, she'd leave the door unguarded. He might walk out before she'd had her say. She moved quickly.

Setting the cup and saucer down as well, she took Reilly's hand and tugged, shamelessly using one of Aurora's tactics—sheer force of will. "Come on. I'll show you."

She got him as far as the bedroom door. He tossed a

disdainful glance at the bed, the comforter Cook had made him, the bright watercolors Melissa had hung on the walls, the dresser in the corner. His dresser.

Behind him she folded her arms, making her stand. "I take it you didn't stop in your room before coming out here to yell at me."

He hadn't had time. He'd been away from her for a month, dreaming of her, living for this day. Which was why it hit him like the concussion following a blast when Cook told him she'd moved out to the cottage. Cook hadn't said *what* she'd moved out to the cottage.

He turned slowly on his heel.

Melissa raised her chin, a fighter who'd foolishly, brazenly lowered her guard. She had absolutely no sense of self-protection left. She didn't need it anymore. "I know you like things in their place. This is their place."

"You moved my bedroom out here?"

"This is where you belong. With me."

He couldn't make his hands take her in his arms. He needed a moment for this to sink in. The cottage had special meaning for him too. It was the place he'd first made love to her; the place he'd almost blown it by holding himself back. He didn't want to ruin his chance again. He wouldn't get another.

FOURTEEN

He strode to the center of the living room, scanning the fireplace, the antique andirons she must've borrowed from the blue bedroom in the east wing, a chair and an ottoman he recognized from the west wing. The place was made up of bits and pieces of Bedford House, pieces of his life, paintings from hers, everything reassembled in Melissa's artful way so they all came together, they all belonged.

A little too artfully arranged, he decided on second thought. Having never had a home to call her own, she'd made this one a picture-perfect ideal of the vine-covered cottage. And she'd done it for them. "You expect us to live together. Is that it?"

"Not exactly." She walked up to him, toe to toe, face-to-face.

The bravery some women had to have, he thought.

"After addressing all those invitations to Helene's friends, the women with their husband's names crossed out, the husbands with new wives added, changes of address, country, marital status, it only reinforced my belief that wedding vows are no guarantee that love will last."

"They're a start," he said with a growl.

"Then I'm ready to start."

He eyed her warily. "You'll marry me?"

"On one condition."

He huffed, turning angrily aside. "That isn't marriage."

She sat daintily at the table, crossing her long legs. She picked up the teapot and poured. Using faintly tarnished silver tongs borrowed from the main kitchen, she plopped two cubes of sugar into his cup.

He grunted and sat down. Dispensing with the tongs, he dropped two more sugars in his cup. He had a feeling he'd need them.

Glancing over her cup's rim, she sipped. "Still love me?"

"A month hasn't changed that."

"Love means accepting people the way they are."

"Meaning the little girl comes before me."

"She did come before."

"I have to know you're mine."

"I am."

"Until Helene and Reggie break up."

Melissa spread her fingers on the blue-and-white checks of the tablecloth. "If they last five years, we'll be home free. Aurora needs to grow up a little more, that's all. I'm only asking you to wait."

"Let me see if I've got this straight. I get five years of provisional marriage with the option to make it permanent once the child's grown." He muttered a curse, shaking his head.

"We can make it work. I'll marry you."

"For the time being. There's not a vow written that comes with an escape clause. Exceptin' of course His Lordship's prenuptial agreement with your mistress. She was happy enough to sign that."

"She's been burned before."

"So have we all. We can't hang our lives on how their marriage goes."

They stared at their cups of tea. She sipped hers as if a sudden move would scald her lips. He downed his in a gulp. He wanted to drag her in his arms, not sit there negotiating as if this were some cease-fire agreement.

"People left you," he said. "They deserted you because they fell in love with someone else. I'm not goin' anywhere, Melissa. Ever. Can't you give me a similar promise?"

"Not without breaking another one."

Another long silence. Another quiet plea. "Don't make me choose, Reilly."

"Looks as if you already have." He rose, more tired than he'd ever felt. Turning to go, he kicked up a corner of the old carpet she'd used. Taking care of her had become a habit he didn't think he'd ever lose. "There's a better one in the west attic. I'll have it brought over next week."

"Reilly."

He stopped in the doorway. "Yes, Miss?"

Her lips thinned. "I've made this my home. I'll stick with it."

"Unless? Until?" He turned to the closed door, scraping the side of his fist down the rough plaster. His exhortation to Reggie echoed in his mind. *Fight for her. If that doesn't work, try something else. If you love her, don't ever give up*. He wasn't giving up. He just had no idea what to do next. She'd promised to be there for the child. Could he really begrudge her that?

His head came up when a flash of color outside caught his eye. Aurora ran down the path toward the cottage. She stopped to pluck a flower first. Reilly watched her raise it to her lips, sniffing with all her might. She caught sight of him through the window and waved, delaying her visit to wade into a crowd of lilies of the valley. "Aurora's coming."

Melissa said nothing.

This was the way it would be if he accepted her proposal. Aurora coming to Melissa and Melissa being there. Why not? he thought. Why couldn't they manage? He turned. "You promised you'd always be there for the child."

"You know I did."

"Then why can't you be *here* for her?"

"Here?" She looked up at him.

"If anything happened with her parents, you'd be here. With me. She'd know where you were. She'd know she was always welcome."

"It wouldn't be the same."

"Why don't you ask her?"

"How could I ask her that? She's a child."

"Ask if she minds us marrying."

Melissa scoffed at his blunt demand. "You know what she'd say. She'd love it; it would mean more woo. To her it'd be another chance to wear her red velvet dress."

"Exactly. She doesn't feel threatened by us being in love. To her it's not a betrayal. She isn't you, Melissa."

No, she wasn't. Drawn to the window, Melissa looked out at the child playing off the path. Aurora wasn't fragile, she was resilient and adaptive and accepting. Melissa knew that. In some way she'd always known it. Still, her job had consisted of making sure Aurora never found out what it meant to be vulnerable, deserted by the people who should have loved her. "She may be a stronger child than I was, but that doesn't mean she can't be hurt."

Reilly stepped up behind her, his voice urgent and low. "She's strong because of you. In all the upheaval of her mother's life, she's always had you. You made her secure enough to deal with this. Ask her. Ask her how *she* feels."

He opened the cottage door the moment Aurora lifted her tiny fist to knock.

"Reilly," she said formally.

"Princess." He bowed deep.

She hugged his neck hard then flounced across the threshold. "I did what you said."

"What was that, lass?"

"I called Mummy in London."

"Long-distance?" Melissa asked.

"Cook helped. I wanted an answer to my letter."

"Which letter was that?"

"The one I wrote myself." Supremely pleased with herself, she strolled around the cottage.

All the same, those dancing blue eyes wouldn't meet Melissa's. "Aurora?"

"Reilly said I should," she blurted out.

Melissa fixed him with a no-nonsense stare. "Okay, what's up?"

"The moment I walked in the house, she was on me about that letter," Reilly replied. "I suggested she call her mother if she couldn't wait until tomorrow."

Melissa glanced at her haughty little charge. She easily pictured Aurora making demands on Reilly the moment he came home; she'd inherited that serene sense of entitlement from her mother. Aurora wasn't shy about asking for what she wanted.

No, she wasn't, Melissa thought again. She bounced back, defeats were temporary. When it came to love, Aurora saw herself as entitled to that too. It would never occur to her that love depended on behaving or keeping quiet or staying out of her mother's way. She'd never been burned the way Melissa had. But could Melissa protect her forever? Or had she already protected her long enough to produce a confident, happy child?

Sitting at her desk by the window, Aurora pulled out paper and pencils as if preparing to write a follow-up to her mysterious letter.

Melissa folded her arms. "Which letter would this be?"

"The one about school," the child carelessly replied.

Too carelessly. An uneasy shiver inched up her spine. "You told them about our schoolhouse?" Melissa prompted.

"I told them I wanted to go to school. A real school."

Stunned, Melissa glanced at Reilly. His tactful withdrawal raised the hair on the back of her neck. "School."

Aurora clutched a pencil sharpener in her tiny fist, grinding her pencil to a perfect point. "I want to go. I'm big enough. You said I was smart enough. I didn't get an answer to my letter, so Reilly said call Mummy."

Melissa lowered herself into a chair beside the table. Reilly anticipated her need and pulled it out. "And Mummy said?"

"She said okay. I get to go to public school in September."

Public school, Melissa thought frantically. In England that meant private school. "Boarding school."

"I'd be home on weekends." She dropped the sharpener in the desk and lowered the lid. Setting her papers in a row, she began to draw capital letters. *A B C.* "It'll be fun."

It felt like the end of the world. Melissa's lungs felt empty, her ears buzzed. Slowly she raised her eyes to Reilly's. "You knew."

"I assumed you helped her write it."

"Miss says I'm advanced," Aurora added.

"Aye, you are." He turned to Melissa. "His Lordship and your lady discussed it at dinner one evening after the letter arrived—"

"—and asked your opinion no doubt!" Melissa rounded on him, her fingers clutched furiously in her lap. "You arranged this, too, didn't you? You arranged everything."

His expression hardened. "I suggested a full-time boarding school would be too much for one so young."

"Young? She's only five years old!"

"Almost six," Aurora piped up. "The duke's son is seven and he spends most of the year away at school. He says school is fun."

Melissa propped her elbows on the table, her head in her hands. She hadn't stopped hearing about the seven-year-old ring bearer since the wedding ceremony. "School isn't fun," she declared.

Aurora blinked in mild surprise. "I thought you were smart."

"It isn't a question of being smart! It's being sent away. It's not being wanted—" She stopped herself. Not for the world would she communicate her fears to the child. "Aurora, do you feel unwanted here? Do you want to go to school because your Mummy's found someone else?"

She shrugged. Adults asked the silliest questions. "School is fun."

"Bedford House has been fun, hasn't it?"

"They'll both be fun. I'll be home on weekends and holidays and summer. We can play then if you want."

Melissa rose unsteadily from her chair. Good Lord, she was even wringing her hands. She strode into the kitchen and stared at the crowded shelves without seeing them. She was a wreck and all because Aurora wanted to go to school. She'd *known* Aurora wanted this. The child had talked of nothing else for weeks.

"I think Miss needs a little time to herself, lass. Why don't you play outside?"

Sensing it was time to leave the grown-ups, Aurora got down off her chair and headed toward the door. Clutching paper and pencils to her chest, she halted on the threshold. She turned and paced cautiously into the kitchen. "I'm sorry it was a secret. I knew you wouldn't want me to go, so I didn't tell you." It was that simple.

Melissa laughed dryly, her lungs aching, her smile stiff. Five years old, almost six, and she had her nanny down cold. "It'll be okay, puppet. We'll talk about it later."

"Mummy said it was all right," Aurora added, unable to resist one more plug.

"I'm sure she did. Go outside now."

She reached out to touch Aurora's hair, but the child was already heading back to the living room. Melissa's hand lingered in the air.

Reilly opened and closed the door. The little girl

skipped down the path, the tension of the cottage instantly forgotten.

"School," Melissa whispered.

"We're too far from a proper school to take her every day. Boarding's the best idea."

"It's a terrible idea." She whirled on him. "Don't you see what they're doing? They haven't been married a month and they're farming her out. Getting rid of her! She'll be crushed when she realizes."

"She asked to go."

"She sensed she wasn't wanted. I should have paid more attention."

Reilly took her by the arms and shook her. "Listen to yourself. Listen to her. This isn't a rejection, it's an adventure. She wants this. None of the servants have children. She needs to be around other children."

"But *I* need *her*." The broken words barely escaped before the tears fell. Melissa's whole body shook, her breath coming in sobs.

Reilly took her in his arms, stroking her hair, feeling her body quake. "You wanted her to be happy and healthy and strong. You wanted her to handle anything life threw her way. You succeeded. You can take credit for that."

Her eyes blurring with tears, she hardly saw it that way. "I've made her confident enough to get along fine without me, is that it?"

"Is there anything wrong with that?"

Nothing, if she didn't mind being left behind. Again. But Reilly was there. Reilly was handing her his handkerchief, holding her in his arms, letting her cry her fool head off over something as basic and normal as a child going to school. "I can't believe I'm making a fool of myself over this."

"I wouldn't say that, Miss."

"She *wants* to go to school."

"That's what she said."

"She's not scared. She doesn't feel the least bit rejected."

"Thanks to you."

"I *have* done a good job."

"You have at that."

"So why am I miserable?" she wailed.

He tipped her chin up. "You're a woman, aren't you?"

A woman's fist thudded weakly against his biceps. "Don't start that again."

"She's a chick leaving the nest. You hate to lose her. That's normal enough. Children grow up."

"I just didn't want her to grow up so soon. And school!"

"What's wrong with that, then?"

She swiped at her nose with the handkerchief. She didn't have to think long. "When I was fourteen my mother married for the fifth time. She announced they were sending me off to school. Boarding school. It wasn't a temporary visit with my father, it was exile. I never felt so rejected. I look back on it, it's silly now. But it hurt. It meant I wasn't wanted."

"I want you. Aurora wants you. She'll still need you."

Melissa rapidly dabbed her tears when the little girl stuck her head in the door. "What is it, puppet?"

"Are you done arguing?"

Melissa pulled out a chair and sat down, extending

her arms. Aurora raced into them. Melissa rocked her gently, petting her hair.

"Don't feel bad, Miss."

"It's not me I'm worried about." Melissa tried not to hold too tight, really she did. "I'll always be here, puppet. No matter what happens, you know that."

"Where else would you go?"

Reilly gently smeared a tear off Melissa's cheek with the backs of his fingers. "That's right, lass. She'll always be here for you."

"With you, Reilly?" she asked.

"Aye," he answered. "If she'll have me."

"She loves you. Oops. She told me not to tell you."

"Then it'll be our secret."

Aurora giggled. Outside, a butterfly drifted on the late-summer breeze, beckoning. She squirmed off Melissa's lap. "May I?"

"Go ahead."

"You aren't going to cry anymore?"

"I'm fine."

She kissed Melissa's cheek. Then she slipped a flower with a broken stem in Reilly's hand. "More woo," she whispered.

"Thanks, lass."

Melissa rolled her eyes, but it was no use pretending. The moment Aurora was gone she longed to be in his arms. She needed someone to lean on, someone like Reilly who always knew how to make things right. She wrapped her arms around him, pressing her cheek against the warmth of his throat. "She doesn't need me anymore."

"She knows where to find you if she does." He kissed

her hair, her cheek, the tangy moisture of her tears. "If she doesn't need you, I do."

"You don't need anyone. You're Reilly. The world runs because you wind up the clocks every morning."

"A man doesn't need a woman the way a child does." He kissed her soft and slow, making his intentions clear. "But if it's another child you want, one to raise fearless and confident and well-loved, I think that can be arranged. There's no better corner of the world to raise one in."

No better place because Reilly made it so—safe, cared for, protected. Melissa looked around the cottage. This might be a small corner of the estate, but it was theirs. She took some of the credit for that. "You want to live here?"

"I want to marry thee."

"That doesn't sound like a question."

"It isn't."

She huffed a shocked laugh. "You're usually a little more tactful, Mr. Reilly. I'd thought you'd ask me formally."

An urgency she knew well burned in his eyes. "You belong here. With me. There's no question about it."

"Do I have a say in this?"

"If it's yes."

She touched his face, tracing the fine scar from his temple to his ear. She'd never trusted love, never trusted anyone with her emotions. But Reilly was another matter. She'd trusted him with her life the day she got on that helicopter. She'd trusted him with her body on more than one night. She trusted him to take her love and keep it safe. As long as Reilly was in charge, everything would work out fine.

"How do you do that?" she asked, marveling. "Make me believe in things, take risks? You even got me in that glorified eggbeater of yours."

"And I'll get thee to an altar yet."

She curved into his arms. "And if Helene and Reggie's marriage doesn't last?"

"Ours will."

Another kiss. He'd told her once that every act of love was a promise. He made promises.

So did she.

"You can stay here and work, paint, have children, and love me. If the little girl needs you, she'll know where to find you."

"And you?"

"What about me?"

She parted her lips and let him enter, tasting him, savoring him. "Will you ever need me the way I need you?"

"I'll love you until this house crumbles around us."

With Reilly to look after it, it never would.

"I love you, Reilly."

"You believe it, then?"

"I believe in you."

It was all he needed to hear. He opened the door and shouted to Aurora. "Your riding lesson's been moved to one o'clock, lass. You best get moving."

The child shrieked and raced toward the stables.

Melissa smiled, twining her arms around his neck. "You had that arranged before you came here."

"I like to think ahead."

"You think of everything."

"I think of you. I can't imagine I'll ever stop."

He closed the door softly behind him. Melissa held

her breath until he was in her arms. They kissed and murmured a hundred promises. The words didn't matter, the vows did. She'd finally found what she'd missed all her life, a love to believe in. Reilly was passionate and urgent in her arms; he was also sure and steady, patient and knowing. His love was a solid foundation on which to build a home. It was time to begin.

COMING SOON— LOVESWEPT'S TREASURED TALES III CONTEST!!!

TOP TEN REASONS TO ENTER LOVESWEPT'S TREASURED TALES III CONTEST:

10) You don't have to worry about it until our February '95 Treasured Tales III Loveswepts are available (on sale January).

9) You can brush up on your Trivial Pursuit skills.

8) It's a great way to relax after the invasion of annoying family members during the holidays.

7) It's the perfect thing to do while polishing off the leftover fudge, divinity and fruitcake.

6) It's more fun than sticking to New Year's resolutions.

5) It'll help you avoid the post-holiday blues.

4) It'll take you to London, a Southern plantation, the theater, and Paradise!

3) Glenna McReynolds, Peggy Webb, Patt Bucheister, and Victoria Leigh.

2) You need another reason?

1) PRIZES, FUN AND MORE PRIZES!!!

THE EDITOR'S CORNER

What better way to celebrate the holidays than with four terrific new LOVESWEPTs! And this month we are excited to present you with romances that are full of passion, humor, and most of all, true love—everything that is best about this time of year. So sit back and indulge yourself in the magic of the season.

Starting things off is the fabulous Mary Kay Mc-Comas with **PASSING THROUGH MIDNIGHT**, LOVESWEPT #722. Gil Howlett believes all women are mysteries, but he *has* to discover what has driven Dorie Devries into hiding in his hometown! Struggling with old demons, Dorie wonders if deep sorrow ever heals, but Gil's tenderness slowly wins her trust. Now he must soothe the wounded spirit of this big-city doctor who challenges him to believe in forgotten dreams. Heartwarming and heartbreaking,

Mary Kay's novels weave a marvelous tapestry of emotions into stories you wish would never end.

The wonderfully talented Debra Dixon wants to introduce you to **DOC HOLIDAY,** LOVESWEPT #723. Drew Haywood needs an enchantress to help give his son a holiday to remember—and no one does Christmas better than Taylor Bishop! She can transform a house into a home that smells of gingerbread and sparkles with tinsel, and kissing her is like coming out of the cold. She's spent her whole life caring for others, but when sweet temptation beckons, this sexy family man must convince her to break all her rules. With poignant humor and sizzling sensuality, Debra has crafted an unforgettable story of the magic of Christmas.

The ever-popular Adrienne Staff returns with **SPELLBOUND,** LOVESWEPT #724. Edward Rockford sees her first in the shadows and senses the pretty artist somehow holds the key to his secrets—but when he enters Jamie Payton's loft, he is stunned to discover that her painting reveals what he's hidden from all the world. Haunted by ghosts from the past, Jamie yearns to share his sanctuary. But can his seductive sorcery set her free? Conjured of equal parts destiny and mystery, passion and emotion, Adrienne's stories capture the imagination and compel the heart to believe once more in a love for all time.

Last but never least is Susan Connell with **RINGS ON HER FINGERS,** LOVESWEPT #725. She really knows how to fill her Christmas stockings, Steve Stratton decides with admiration at first sight of the long-legged brunette dressed as a holiday elf! Gwen Mansfield feels her heart racing like a runaway sleigh when the gorgeous architect invites her to play under his tree—and vows to be good. A jinxed love life has made her wary, but maybe Steve is the one to change her luck. Susan Connell has always written about intrepid heroes and damsels in just enough distress to make life interesting, but now she delivers the perfect Christmas present, complete with surprises and glittering fun!

Happy reading!

With best wishes,

Beth de Guzman

Beth de Guzman

Senior Editor

P.S. Don't miss the exciting women's novels that are coming your way from Bantam in January! **HEAVEN'S PRICE,** from blockbuster author Sandra Brown, is a classic romantic novel in hardcover for the first time; **LORD OF ENCHANTMENT,** by bestselling author Suzanne Robinson, is an enchanting tale of romance and intrigue on a stormy isle off the coast of Elizabethan England; **SURRENDER TO A STRANGER,** by Karyn Monk, is an utterly compelling, passionately romantic debut from an exceptionally talented new historical romance author. We'll be giving you a sneak peek at these terrific books in next month's LOVESWEPTs. And immediately following this page look for a preview of the exciting romances from Bantam that are *available now!*

Don't miss these sensational books by
your favorite Bantam authors

On sale in November

ADAM'S FALL
by Sandra Brown

PURE SIN
by Susan Johnson

ON WINGS OF MAGIC
by Kay Hooper

ADAM'S FALL

by

SANDRA
BROWN

"Ms. Brown's larger than life heroes and heroines
make you believe all the warm, wonderful,
wild things in life."
—*Rendezvous*

BLOCKBUSTER AUTHOR SANDRA BROWN—
WHOSE NAME IS ALMOST SYNONYMOUS
WITH *THE NEW YORK TIMES* BEST-
SELLER LIST—OFFERS A CLASSIC ROMAN-
TIC NOVEL THAT ACHES WITH EMOTION
AND SIZZLES WITH PASSION. . . .

They still fought like cats and dogs, but their relationship drastically improved.

He still cursed her, accused her of being heartless
out of pure meanness, and insisted that she pushed
him beyond his threshold of pain and endurance.

She still cursed him and accused him of being a

gutless rich kid who, for the first time in his charmed life, was experiencing hardship.

He said she couldn't handle patients worth a damn.

She said he couldn't handle adversity worth a damn.

He said she taunted him unmercifully.

She said he whined incessantly.

And so it went. But things were definitely better.

He came to trust her just a little. He began to listen when she told him that he wasn't trying hard enough and should put more concentration into it. And he listened when she advised that he was trying too hard and needed to rest awhile.

"Didn't I tell you so?" She was standing at the foot of his bed, giving therapy to his ankle.

"I'm still not ready to tap dance."

"But you've got sensation."

"You stuck a straight pin into my big toe!"

"But you've got sensation." She stopped turning his foot and looked up toward the head of his bed, demanding that he agree.

"I've got sensation." The admission was grumbled, but he couldn't hide his pleased smile.

"In only two and a half weeks." She whistled. "You've come a long way, baby. I'm calling Honolulu today and ordering a set of parallel bars. You'll soon be able to stand between them."

His smile collapsed. "I'll never be able to do that."

"That's what you said about the wheelchair. Will you lighten up?"

"Will you?" He grunted with pain as she bent his knee back toward his chest.

"Not until you're walking."

"If you keep wearing those shorts, I'll soon be running. I'll be chasing you."

"Promises, promises."

"I thought I told you to dress more modestly."

"This is Hawaii, Cavanaugh. Everybody goes casual, or haven't you heard? I'm going to resist the movement now. Push against my hand. That's it. A little harder. Good."

"Ah, God," he gasped through clenched teeth. He followed her instructions, which took him through a routine to stretch his calf muscle. "The backs of your legs are sunburned," he observed as he put forth even greater effort.

"You noticed?"

"How could I help it? You flash them by me every chance you get. Think those legs of yours are long enough? They must start in your armpits. But how'd I get off on that? What were we talking about?"

"Why my legs were sunburned. Okay, Adam, let up a bit, then try it again. Come on now, no ugly faces. One more time." She picked up the asinine conversation in order to keep his mind off his discomfort. "My legs are sunburned because I fell asleep beside the pool yesterday afternoon."

"Is that what you're being paid an exorbitant amount of money to do? To nap beside my swimming pool?"

"Of course not!" After a strategic pause, she added, "I went swimming too." He gave her a baleful look and pressed his foot against the palm of her hand. "Good, Adam, good. Once more."

"You said that was the last one."

"I lied."

"You heartless bitch."

"You gutless preppy."

Things were swell.

"Susan Johnson brings sensuality to new heights
and beyond."
—*Romantic Times*

Susan Johnson

NATIONALLY BESTSELLING AUTHOR
OF *SEIZED BY LOVE* AND *OUTLAW*

PURE SIN

*From the erotic imagination of bestselling author Susan
Johnson comes a tale of exquisite pleasure that begins in the
wilds of Montana—and ends in the untamed places of two
lovers' hearts.*

"A shame we didn't ever meet," Adam said with a
seductive smile, his responses automatic with beautiful women. "Good conversation is rare."

She didn't suppose most women were interested
exclusively in his conversation, Flora thought, as she
took in the full splendor of his dark beauty and
power. Even lounging in a chair, his legs casually
crossed at the ankles, he presented an irresistible image of brute strength. And she'd heard enough rumor
in the course of the evening to understand he enjoyed
women—nonconversationally. "As rare as marital fi-
delity no doubt."

His brows rose fractionally. "No one's had the
nerve to so bluntly allude to my marriage. Are you

speaking of Isolde's or my infidelities?" His grin was boyish.

"Papa says you're French."

"Does that give me motive or excuse? And I'm only half French, as you no doubt know, so I may have less excuse than Isolde. She apparently prefers Baron Lacretelle's properties in Paris and Nice to my dwelling here."

"No heartbroken melancholy?"

He laughed. "Obviously you haven't met Isolde."

"Why did you marry then?"

He gazed at her for a moment over the rim of the goblet he'd raised to his lips. "You can't be that naive," he softly said, then quickly drained the glass.

"Forgive me. I'm sure it's none of my business."

"I'm sure it's not." The warmth had gone from his voice and his eyes. Remembering the reason he'd married Isolde always brought a sense of chaffing anger.

"I haven't felt so gauche in years," Flora said, her voice almost a whisper.

His black eyes held hers, their vital energy almost mesmerizing, then his look went shuttered and his grin reappeared. "How could you know, darling? About the idiosyncrasies of my marriage. Tell me now about your first sight of Hagia Sophia."

"It was early in the morning," she began, relieved he'd so graciously overlooked her faux pas. "The sun had just begun to appear over the crest of the—"

"Come dance with me," Adam abruptly said, leaning forward in his chair. "This waltz is a favorite of mine," he went on, as though they hadn't been discussing something completely different. Reaching over, he took her hands in his. "And I've been want-ing to"—his hesitation was minute as he discarded the inappropriate verb—"hold you." He grinned. "You see how blandly circumspect my choice of words is." Rising, he gently pulled her to her feet. "Considering the newest scandal in my life, I'm on my best behavior tonight."

"But then scandals don't bother me." She was standing very close to him, her hands still twined in his.

His fine mouth, only inches away, was graced with a genial smile and touched with a small heated play-fulness. "I thought they might not."

"When one travels as I do, one becomes inured to other people's notions of nicety." Her bare shoulders lifted briefly, ruffling the limpid lace on her décolle-tage. He noticed both the pale satin of her skin and the tantalizing swell of her bosom beneath the deli-cate lace. "If I worried about scandal," she murmured with a small smile, "I'd never set foot outside En-gland."

"And you do."

"Oh yes," she whispered. And for a moment both were speaking of something quite different.

"You're not helping," he said in a very low voice. "I've sworn off women for the moment."

"To let your wounds heal?"

"Nothing so poetical." His quirked grin reminded her of a teasing young boy. "I'm reassessing my pri-orities."

"Did I arrive in Virginia City too late then?"

"Too late?" One dark brow arched infinitesimally.

"To take advantage of your former priorities."

He took a deep breath because he was already perversely aware of the closeness of her heated body, of the heady fragrance of her skin. "You're a bold young lady, Miss Bonham."

"I'm twenty-six years old, Mr. Serre, and independent."

"I'm not sure after marriage to Isolde that I'm interested in any more willful aristocratic ladies."

"Perhaps I could change your mind."

He thoughtfully gazed down at her, and then the faintest smile lifted the graceful curve of his mouth. "Perhaps you could."

"[Kay Hooper] writes with exceptional
beauty and grace."
—*Romantic Times*

Kay Hooper

NATIONALLY BESTSELLING AUTHOR OF
THE WIZARD OF SEATTLE

ON WINGS OF MAGIC

*One of today's most beloved romance authors, Kay Hooper
captivates readers with the wit and sensuality of her work.
Now the award-winning writer offers a passionate story
filled with all the humor and tenderness her fans have
come to expect—a story that explores the loneliness of
heartbreak and the searing power of love. . . .*

"Tell me, Kendall—why the charade?"

"Why not?" She looked at him wryly. "I am what
people expect me to be."

"You mean men."

"Sure. Oh, I could rant and rave about not being
valued for who I am instead of what I look like, but
what good would that do? My way is much easier.
And there's no harm done."

"I don't know about that." Seriously, he went on,
"By being what people expect you to be, you don't
give anyone the chance to see the real you."

Interested in spite of herself, she frowned thoughtfully. "But how many people really care what's beneath the surface, Hawke? Not many," she went on, answering her own question. "We all act out roles we've given ourselves, pretend to be things we're not—or things we want to be. And we build walls around the things we want to hide."

"What do you want to hide, Kendall?" he asked softly.

Ignoring the question, she continued calmly. "It's human nature. We want to guess everyone else's secrets without giving our own away."

"And if someone wants to see beneath the surface?"

Kendall shrugged. "We make them dig for it. You know—make them prove themselves worthy of our trust. Of all the animals on this earth, we're the most suspicious of a hand held out in friendship."

Hawke pushed his bowl away and gazed at her with an oddly sober gleam in his eyes. "Sounds like you learned that lesson the hard way," he commented quietly.

She stared at him, surprise in her eyes, realizing for the first time just how cynical she'd become. Obeying some nameless command in his smoky eyes, she said slowly, "I've seen too much to be innocent, Hawke. Whatever ideals I had . . . died long ago."

He stared at her for a long moment, then murmured, "I think I'd better find a pick and a shovel."

Suddenly angry with her own burst of self-revelation, Kendall snapped irritably, "Why?"

"To dig beneath the surface." He smiled slowly. "You're a fascinating lady, Kendall James. And I think

. . . if I dig deep enough . . . I just might find gold."

"What you might find," she warned coolly, "is a booby trap. I'm not a puzzle to be solved, Hawke."

"Aren't you? You act the sweet innocent, telling yourself that it's the easy way. And it's a good act, very convincing and probably very useful. But it isn't entirely an act, is it, honey? There is an innocent inside of you, hiding from the things she's seen."

"You're not a psychologist and I'm not a patient, so stop with the analyzing," she muttered, trying to ignore what he was saying.

"You're a romantic, an idealist," he went on as if she hadn't spoken. "But you hide that part of your nature—behind a wall that isn't a wall at all. You've got yourself convinced that it's an act, and that conviction keeps you from being hurt."

Kendall shot him a glare from beneath her lashes. "Now you're not even making sense," she retorted scornfully.

"Oh, yes, I am." His eyes got that hooded look she was beginning to recognize out of sheer self-defense. "A piece of the puzzle just fell into place. But it's still a long way from being solved. And, rest assured, Kendall, I intend to solve it."

"Is this in the nature of another warning?" she asked lightly, irritated that her heart had begun to beat like a jungle drum.

"Call it anything you like."

"I could just leave, you know."

"You could." The heavy lids lifted, revealing a cool challenge. "But that would be cowardly."

Knowing—*knowing*—that she was walking right

into his trap, Kendall snapped, "I'm a lot of things, Hawke, but a coward isn't one of them!" And felt strongly tempted to throw her soup bowl at him when she saw the satisfaction that flickered briefly in his eyes.

"Good," he said briskly. "Then we can forget about that angle, can't we? And get down to business."

"Business?" she murmured wryly. "That's one I haven't heard."

"Well, I would have called it romance, but I didn't want you to laugh at me." He grinned faintly. "Men are more romantic than women, you know. I read it somewhere."

"Fancy that." Kendall stared at him. "Most of the men I've known let romance go by the board."

"Really? Then knowing me will be an education."

Don't miss these fabulous Bantam women's fiction titles

Now On Sale

ADAM'S FALL
by *New York Times* bestselling author
Sandra Brown

Blockbuster author Sandra Brown—whose name is almost synonymous with the *New York Times* bestseller list—offers a classic romantic novel that aches with emotion and sizzles with passion.
❏ *56768-3 $4.99/$5.99 in Canada*

PURE SIN
by nationally bestselling author
Susan Johnson

From the erotic imagination of Susan Johnson comes a tale of exquisite pleasure that begins in the wilds of Montana—and ends in the untamed places of two lovers' hearts.
❏ *29956-5 $5.50/6.99 in Canada*

ON WINGS OF MAGIC
by award-winning author
Kay Hooper

Award-winning Kay Hooper offers a passionate story filled with all the humor and tenderness her fans have come to expect—a story that explores the loneliness of heartbreak and the searing power of love.
❏ *56965-1 $4.99/$5.99 in Canada*